Free Spirit

"Lizzie, I would appreciate it if you would give me a leave of absence." Dory laid her written request on the desk and waited for Lizzie to say something.

"Why?" It was a question, a demand, a don't give me any crap answer.

Dory swallowed hard. "I want to work on my doctorate."

Lizzie leaned across the desk. "Does this have anything to do with Griff? Level with me, Dory."

"I'm going to be moving in with him. I'll be attending Georgetown, so it will work out all around."

"You think so, do you, Dory? What if I told you I was leaving here in six months and planned on having you step into my job? What would you say to that?"

"I'd be stunned," Dory said truthfully.

"Well," said Lizzie. "I want you to promise me something. I want you to call me in three months and tell me how it looks from where you are. You owe me that."

Dory agreed, even though she had no idea how she'd feel in three months . . .

Fern Michaels

For the past nine years, Mary Kuczkir and Roberta Anderson have pooled their energies, talents, and imaginations to write twenty-one books, all of which have been successfully published under their carefully chosen pen name ("Fern" for the plastic tree in Mary's living room that resembled a fern; "Michaels" after her husband and son). They are the authors of the best-selling historical romances CAPTIVE INNOCENCE and TENDER WARRIOR, as well as the contemporary LOVE & LIFE novel ALL SHE CAN BE.

"Are we rich, successful authors and shrewd businesswomen?" the New Jersey duo asks. "You bet we are! We never stop learning. It's what we do best. Each day we work harder to perfect our craft and to write the best book possible. But we're still wives, mothers (Mary is a grandmother), cooks, nurses, gardeners, and chauffeurs. When people ask who we are, we say we're Mary and Roberta. Fern Michaels is what we do, not who we are."

Fern Michaels

Free Spirit

BALLANTINE BOOKS • NEW YORK

Library of Congress Catalog Card Number: 83-90017

ISBN 0-345-30840-9

Manufactured in the United States of America

First Edition: September 1983

Chapter One

ONLY THE RUSTLING OF THEIR BODIES AGAINST THE SHEETS AND the soft sounds of their murmurings broke the silence of the night. She nestled against him, burrowing her head into the hollow of his neck, the silky strands of her pale blonde hair falling over his shoulder. She breathed the scent of him, mingled with the fragrance of her own perfume. Her fingers teased the light furring of his chest hairs; her leg, thrown intimately over his, felt the lean, sinewy muscles of his thigh.

They were like light and shadow—she silvered, the color of moonlight, and he dark, like the night. He held her, gentle hands soothing her, bringing her back down from erotic heights.

It was the best of all times, this moment after making love, when all barriers were down and satiny skin melted into masculine hardness. This closeness was the true communion of lovers who had brought peace and satisfaction to one another.

Dory Faraday burrowed deeper into the nest of Griff's embrace. He drew her closer and she smiled. She loved this hunk, as she liked to call him. He was good for her in every way—understanding her and accepting her for the person she was.

"Want to talk about it?" Griff asked softly, as his fingers traced lazy patterns up her arm.

"I suppose we should. It's just that this is such a perfect

1

moment, and I hate to tamper with perfection.'' She felt his smile through the darkness. They had discussed Griff's leaving New York for months, but now that the time had almost arrived, Dory was finding it hard to accept. Washington, D.C. was only forty-five minutes away by air, but this knowledge did not bring her comfort. Holding tightly to Griff, Dory whispered, ''This is our last day. I'm going to miss you until it's time for me to join you. Up to now, everything has been so perfect. We had our work, our careers . . .'' She stopped to dab at her eyes with the hem of the lavender-scented sheet.

''Shhh. Don't cry, Dory.'' His touch was comforting as he wiped away her tears with the tips of his fingers. ''It's only a few weeks. D.C. is only minutes away, and we can talk on the phone in the evening. You said you understood.'' His wasn't an accusing tone, but Dory felt compelled to move and struggled to prop herself on one elbow to face him.

''I do understand, Griff. It's a golden opportunity for you and you had the idea long before you met me. You deserve this chance. You'll broaden your horizons and do the work you like best. It's just that I'm going to miss you. Simple as that. I also have a few qualms about telling Lizzie I want a leave of absence.''

There was an anxious note in Griff's voice, and he reached to touch the silky strands of Dory's hair, rubbing them between his fingertips. ''You aren't anticipating any problems, are you?'' If he had been in a less romantic position, he would have crossed his fingers. How he loved this long-legged woman with the lithe cougar walk and one hundred sixty-two pairs of shoes. When she offered to take a leave of absence to join him in Washington, he had been more than pleased, but he was also apprehensive. Was it selfish of him to agree that Dory give up her prestigious position at *Soiree* magazine? He admired her independence and didn't want to infringe on her career. Life in D.C. would be different for her but, as she explained, it would also present new opportunities. That had made him feel better, but now he wished, for the thousandth time, that she would accept his proposal of marriage instead of opting for a live-in arrangement. At least he would see more of her in D.C. than here in New York, where Dory lived in her small but stylish apartment while he continued occupying his loft. If things worked out with his new partnership in the veterinary clinic and if Dory could find challenging work, perhaps she would change her mind. Marriage was what Griff really wanted.

"No, honey, I'm not anticipating problems with Lizzie. She's fair and I've worked hard. The magazine can hardly refuse me a leave of absence to pursue my doctorate, can they?" She rushed on, as though not wanting to entertain for one instant the possibility that her request might be refused. "I can do all the freelance work I want from Washington. Contrary to popular opinion, Griff, New York is not the *only* city in the world where a woman can find work. Meaningful work. Even if we live in Alexandria or Arlington, school and work won't be a problem." Her tone was only a shade less anxious than Griff's, and if the room weren't darkened, he would have seen her vivid green eyes cloud with questions. "You aren't having second thoughts, are you, Griff?"

"Good God, no!" He ran his fingers through his thick chestnut hair, the soft waves falling over his wide forehead. "I just want you to be aware of what you're getting into. I'm going to be up to my neck in work for the first couple of months, and our long, lazy weekends are going to come to a screeching halt. The clinic is going to consume me, love. Rick and John are going to be just as busy, so you'll have their wives to keep you company. You're going to be pretty busy, too, going to Georgetown University and keeping house and freelancing. I'll help as much as I can, but I think we should find housekeeping help right off the bat. Don't you?"

Dory pondered the question. "Not right away. Let me settle in and then decide what I can and can't handle. It's going to work out, Griff. Let me take care of the domestic end of things and you concentrate on the veterinary clinic and your partners." She leaned down and found his mouth, delighting in the feel of his lips against hers and the slight abrasiveness of his mustache.

"I should be getting back to the loft." He stretched and

3

squinted at the radium dial of the bedside clock. Three-ten. His eye fell to the floor and the persimmon froth of her discarded nightgown. A lazy look veiled his expression as he lay back down and felt himself stiffening beneath the sheets. What the hell, he could just as easily leave an hour later. This was now and there were some things that would always be more important than sleep. Griff Michaels' Law. He smiled indolently, turning to gather Dory in his arms and nuzzle the softness of her neck.

Dory sensed his immediate mood change and allowed herself to be carried with it. One moment his arms cradled her, soothing her, the next they became her prison, hard, strong, inescapable. She loved him like this, when the wildness flooded his veins and she could feel it beating through him. It brought her a sense of power to know that she could arouse these instincts in him. She yielded to his need for her, welcoming his weight upon her, flexing her thighs to bring him closer.

His hands were in her hair, on her breasts, on the soft flesh of her inner thighs. He stirred her, demanded of her, rewarded her with the adoring attention of his lips to those territories his hands had already claimed. And when he possessed her it was with a joyful abandon that evoked a like response in her: hard, fast, then becoming slower and sweeter.

She murmured her pleasure and gave him those caresses he loved. Release was there, within their grasp, but like two moths romancing a flame, they played in the heat and postponed that exquisite instant when they would plunge into the inferno.

Dory rolled over and stretched luxuriously, feeling vibrant and alive. Griff's vigorous lovemaking always left her ready to conquer worlds and build universes. There was no point in going back to sleep now. She might as well shower and get to the office early after a leisurely breakfast.

A wicked grin stretched across her lips as she watched Griff dress. "You look better in those jockey shorts than Jim Palmer does. Griff, how about doing a layout for *Soiree*?"

Griff laughed. "And have every female who reads that

racy magazine lusting after me? I have all I can do to handle my bills, let alone tons of fan mail. Besides, how would it look to old Mrs. Bettinger when she sees it? God, she'd never bring her cats to me again.''

''Nerd. She isn't going to be bringing her cats to you anymore. You're moving, remember? A head shot? How about one like Burt Reynolds did for *Cosmo*?''

''I can see the headline now: 'Stud Michaels, his own best endorsement.' ''

Dory giggled. ''It would be something to show your grandchildren.''

Griff frowned. She hadn't said ''our'' grandchildren. Immediately he erased the frown. Time. Time would take care of everything.

His kiss was long and lingering. Dory clung to him with a feverishness that surprised him. ''Don't forget we're going to the theatre with my aunt tonight.''

Griff smacked his forehead. ''It's a good thing you reminded me. I forgot all about it.''

''You're going to love Aunt Pixie.''

''The question is, will she love me?''

''She's going to adore you just the way I adore you. If there's one thing Pix is good at, it's sizing up a man. You'll pass muster.''

For a moment Griff wore a frazzled look. ''Dory, all those outrageous things you told me about her. Were they true or were you putting me on? It's not that I care, it's just that I want to be sure to say the right thing to her. I really want her to like me,'' he finished lamely.

''Don't worry. She's going to love you. And, with Pixie you could never do or say the wrong thing. She is outrageous. I used to think everyone had an aunt like her, but she's unique. I don't know what I'd do without her. Anytime I have a problem, she's there. She's been more of a mother to me than my own mother. Look, if you're really worried we could meet in a coffee house for a visit before going on to the theatre. Would that make you feel better?''

Griff nodded.

"Okay, I'll give you a call when we're ready to leave. Now go home and stop worrying. Or are you putting me on and what you're really worried about is this big change in your life?"

Griff grinned. "Lady, you know me too well. Of course I'm concerned. This is a major step in my life. I want it so bad I can taste it, but I still have butterflies when I think about it."

"Go home. Think happy thoughts," Dory said impishly as she pushed him from her. "See you tonight."

He was gone. For a brief moment it seemed as though the walls were going to close in on her, but she recovered quickly. He was gone but it wasn't the end. In more ways than one it was a new beginning. She felt confident, sure of herself and her new choices. Options were something she liked. Options were a part of her life.

Her nakedness was something else she was comfortable with as she padded out to the kitchen to prepare the two-cup coffee pot. She would soak in a nice warm tub and work on her checkbook while the coffee perked. Some French toast for sustenance, and she would be ready to face her day.

The warm, steamy wetness worked its magic as she deftly computed the numbers in her checkbook. It looked good. This month she had an even $200 left that she could invest. She was pleased with the way she had handled her finances. All her bills were paid, money was set aside for the next three weeks for lunches, cab fare, hairdresser, even a new pair of shoes if the mood struck her. She calculated her airline fare into her totals and still she was ahead. Her small portfolio was looking better and better as the months went on. She could exist for an entire year on her savings account alone if she suddenly found herself jobless. Not bad for a career girl who just turned thirty-one.

Dory attacked her breakfast the way she did everything, with energy and gusto, savoring each mouthful. She enjoyed everything about life, more so now that Griff was a part of it. An important job at one of the most prestigious magazines in the country, a wonderful relationship, money in the bank all gave her the confidence she needed to be part of the active life in New York.

She would miss it. But nothing was forever. Now the important thing was being with Griff and taking the proper steps to finish her doctorate.

While the breakfast dishes soaked, Dory poked through her walk-in closet. It was bigger than her tiny living room, and the main reason she had leased the apartment. She finally selected a fawn-colored Albert Nipon original. She loved the feel of the exquisite silk that was one of Nipon's trademarks. She scanned the specially built shelves holding her shoes. The sexy Bruno Magli strap shoe was the perfect choice.

When she left her apartment an hour later she was the epitome of the successful New York career woman. Her lithe cougar walk, as Griff liked to call her long-legged stride, drew more than one admiring glance. She was not unaware of her image, and she reveled in it as she slid gracefully into a cab, returned the driver's smile, and gave the address of *Soiree*.

Dory leaned back and closed her eyes for the ride uptown. Her thoughts were with Griff. Until he came into her life six months ago, she had been so busy carving out a career and seeing to her financial future that she dated rarely, preferring casual relationships that wouldn't get sticky. But all her good intentions fell by the wayside the moment she met Griffin Michaels. It was at a cocktail party given by Oscar de la Renta, and Griff had been dating one of the designer's models. He had looked so elegant in his Brooks Brothers suit and shoes that she had smiled. Loose was the only word that came to her mind at the time. He didn't exactly fit in with that crowd, yet he did. He wasn't impressed, of that she was certain; in fact, he seemed to be bored by all the surface glamour and sophistication. She had taken the initiative and introduced herself. Things progressed rapidly; within the hour he made his apologies to his date, who was hanging onto a male model, and he and Dory left together to have a drink at a small cocktail lounge.

It was a wonderful old-fashioned courtship. Long walks in

Central Park, weekend dates that always ended at her front door at midnight or shortly thereafter. Delicious, searing kisses that left her breathless and wanting more were a way of life for six weeks until he finally seduced her. Or had she seduced him? It didn't matter now. Now they were truly together.

They found they had much in common. They both knew the words to all the Golden Oldies and often danced in her small living room to the beautiful songs. They loved the same writers and laughingly compared books. He loved walking in the rain as much as she did and regarded snow as the most wondrous thing in the world.

He never crowded her, never asked for more than she was prepared to give. He was patient and understanding, and Dory loved him all the more for it.

Wonderful, short, intimate phone calls from Griff in the middle of the day were something she treasured. Her penchant for sending Snoopy cards delighted Griff. He was pleased that Dory would take time out of her busy schedule to shop for just the right card and mail it at just the right moment. Both had laughed in embarrassment when they admitted that not only had they been thumb suckers but blanket holders as well when they were toddlers. Snoopy and his pals were a joy to read about in the Sunday comics over a long lazy breakfast in bed.

The mutual concern they shared was Dory's most prized possession, if emotion could be considered a possession. She adored the tall, loose individual she called Griff. She was never sure how that adoration had turned into love, but one day she woke and looked at the man sleeping beside her and realized she loved him with all her heart. "For all my life," she had whispered softly, so as not to wake him.

Griff proposed after three months. She refused. She wasn't ready to commit herself to something as awesome as marriage. It would have to wait for a while. Griff said he understood, and smiled when she said she didn't want to move in with him or vice versa, not yet. She needed her own space, and so did he, didn't he? Again, he said he understood.

Her friends told her she was a fool. Here he was, hand-some as sin itself, a successful veterinarian with his own practice, money, no strings attaching him to someone else, great potential. But what did they know, with their on-again–off-again romances that left them teary eyed and neurotic? Thanks, but no thanks. Time was on her side, or so she thought. Griff had been honest with her from the beginning, telling her that he would be giving up his New York practice to open a clinic in the Washington, D.C.–Virginia area with two partners. As soon as the clinic was ready, and he esti-mated the work would be finished within four months, he would be leaving. His practice was sold and he was staying on only until the new vet got the hang of things. He had been up front all the way.

"Here you are, miss," the driver said, leaning over the seat. Dory gave him a second dazzling smile that made him grin. "You have a nice day now, you hear," he said in a fatherly tone. Damn, he wished he was thirty years younger. He also wished he had more fares like her. Made your day when a pretty woman smiled. And this one didn't just smile, she beamed. A meaty lady in slacks two sizes too small huffed and puffed her way into his cab. He shrugged. You win some and you lose some. "Where to, lady?"

Soft early-morning sunshine washed across Dory's desk. The stark white paper stood out against the buff-colored blotter. Her request asking for a leave of absence. She still had an hour before her meeting with Lizzie Adams, the managing editor of *Soiree*. Was she gambling with her future? Was she doing the right thing? Or was following Griff to Washington the wrong thing? That was a negative question and negative thoughts had no place in her life. She hadn't gotten where she was by entertaining negative thoughts. The word "no" was one word she simply refused to recognize. She was a positive person all the way.

Dory stood up and met her reflection in the smoky-mirrored wall. She was attractive by some standards, beautiful by others. Chic, elegant, fashionable were compliments paid to her by the staff. But it was those people closest to Dory who realized that her beauty came from within. Serenity, confidence, success were the traits that made Dory Faraday beautiful.

She straightened the soft silk at the neckline of the Nipon dress. Any designer would have gladly dressed Dory just for the pleasure of seeing his creations shown off to perfection. Bruno Magli would have been pleased to see his soft kid shoes worn on such pretty feet. There was no need for jewelry at the long, slender throat, nor elaborate makeup and a styled hairdo. Dory was naturally lovely. In the world of slick sophistication and cosmetic beauty, Dory Faraday was one of a kind.

The hazy gray mirror lost the reflection as Dory turned to scan her surroundings. She was going to miss this peaceful, charming office where she spent so much of her time. Decorated in earth tones with splashes of vibrant color, it lent itself to the serenity that was Dory's trademark at *Soiree*. Emerald ferns graced the corners of the office, wicker baskets and tubs held flowing greenery. Everything in the room, including Dory, blended like a chord in a symphony.

In the space of fifteen minutes Dory took three phone calls, penciled corrections on a lipstick layout, and nixed a model's see-through blouse. She sat back, her hands folded on the desk while the model ranted and raved about the desirability of the tasteless blouse. "The blouse goes," Dory said crisply, "and so do you if you don't wear the one your ad man sent along with your folio. Take it or leave it."

"Okay, okay," the model snapped as she grabbed the offending article from Dory's desk. "You aren't the last word, Miss Faraday," she shot over her shoulder as she made her way to the door.

"I am if you ever want to do another ad for this magazine." There was no mistaking the ring of steel in Dory's voice. The model hesitated a second and then raced from the office. Dory sighed.

"I heard all that," Katy Simmons laughed as she sailed into Dory's office. Katy was Dory's right hand—keeper of the files, confidante, mother hen, provider of low-calorie brownies. She had been with *Soiree* from Day One and was fond of saying that Dory was the only person she could get along with because Dory knew what she was doing and didn't let people walk all over her. "How's it going today? Never mind, you look like someone gave you the moon and the stars for a present. I hate people like you," she grumbled good naturedly. "Just tell me how the hell you manage to look so gorgeous at eight-thirty in the morning with no makeup. It takes me hours and hours and then I always look like I slept in a park and got dragged by a stray dog."

"You're being too hard on yourself, Katy. And I'm not so dumb that I don't know you're fishing for a compliment. Yes, you have gorgeous eyes and, yes, you have a wealth of hair that I would kill for. Now, does that make you feel better?"

"Sort of." Katy sniffed. "Want your schedule?"

"Why not. I just pretend to work around here."

"First, you have a meeting with Lizzie. I allowed forty-five minutes for that. She wanted an hour but I said no way. You're having lunch with two ad men and are they something. Hunks, both of them. Look sharp. You have a two-hour meeting after lunch so don't be late. A layout presentation after the meeting. Somebody from Dior is having a bash, and it would be a good idea if you made an appearance. It was Lizzie's idea—she can't go. She's all booked up with out of town clients who are demanding more space but don't want to pay for it. Some new models are downstairs, modeling jeans. They want you to take a look-see and give them your opinion. I told them you wouldn't be caught dead in jeans but they wouldn't listen. I picked up the two new profiles for the spring issue and they need your pencil and approval. Whenever is okay. Today, if you can. And, if you have any extra time this evening, I have tickets for the theatre that some turkey sent here for you. He said he'd meet you in the lobby at curtain time. I guess that's about it. Now, what do you want *me* to do today? I have this headache and one of my corns is killing me, so take that into consideration when you unload on me."

"Cancel the turkey with the tickets. I'm already going to

the theatre tonight. Go back to the lounge and take a catnap. I can handle things here. Send Susy in and she can take some light dictation I didn't get done yesterday. That's an order, Katy.''

"Yes, Ms. Faraday," Katy drawled as she left the office.

The door opened and a breathless young girl breezed through as though blown on the wind. "Gee, Miss Faraday, do I really get to help you today? Katy said she was too busy. I love that dress and those shoes are out of this world. You're just gorgeous, you really are. Everyone says so. They all talk about you out in the typing pool."

Dory smiled when the girl finished. "Do you know you said that all in one breath? Amazing. Thanks for the compliments, and you can thank the girls in the office for me too. This is what I want you to do." Quickly she outlined the work, ending with instructions to water the plants and make coffee. "I have a meeting with Lizzie and I know she could use some about now. Refer all my calls to her office. Why don't you work here at my desk while I'm gone."

There was reverence in Susy's eyes. Wait till the girls outside heard she was not only working at Dory Faraday's desk but also watering her plants and making coffee. She'd be the talk of the office for a week. Some day she was going to be just like Dory Faraday. She could feel it in her bones.

The plaque on the door read, "Lizzie Adams, Managing Editor." Dory rapped softly and opened the door. She held the stiff paper in her right hand at her side.

"Dory, come in. Coffee?" She looked around vaguely as though expecting it to materialize out of nowhere.

"I told one of the girls to bring some up. It should be ready soon. I've got a full schedule today, Lizzie, so I'll get right to the point. I would appreciate it if you would give me a leave of absence." She laid her written request on the dark green blotter and waited for Lizzie to say something.

Lizzie was a chunk of a woman. From the neck down she was all one size. Pudgy, she called herself. But people never seemed to notice her size; they kept looking at her face. She had eyes the color of warm chocolate and the thickest eyelashes

Dory had ever seen. A flawless complexion and perfect white teeth. Hair that was clipped short and blown back from her face. She looked sixteen while, in fact, she was thirty-six.

"Why?" It was a question, a demand, a don't-give-me-any-crap answer.

Dory swallowed hard. "I want to work on my doctorate."

"Just like that. No warning, no nothing. You just walk in here and ask for time off. I asked you why? How much time?"

Dory stared at Lizzie, not understanding her attitude. They had always gotten along. Why was she being so dogmatic about this? Dory's stomach churned. Lizzie would understand about the doctorate but she would never understand Dory wanting to follow Griff to Washington. No one at *Soiree* would understand something like that. The doctorate really was her main reason for the leave of absence. The timing was perfect; she could live with Griff.

"I told you, Lizzie, to pursue my education until I complete it. That's the best answer I can give you. If you can't hold my job, I'll understand."

Lizzie leaned across the desk. "Does this have anything to do with Griff? Level with me, Dory."

"I'm going to move in with him. I'll be studying at Georgetown, so it will work out all around."

"You think so, do you? If you thought that, why aren't you getting married?"

"I'm not ready for that kind of commitment yet, Lizzie. This is what's best for me right now. For me, Lizzie. No one else."

"What if I told you I was leaving here in six months and planned on having you step into my job? What would you say to that?"

"I'd be stunned," Dory said truthfully, her green eyes widening in surprise.

"Then look stunned. You know, open mouth, insert foot, raise your eyebrows and all that."

"Are you serious?"

"Damn right I'm serious. Who did you think I would pick?"

"I never thought about it. I didn't know you were leaving."

"Jack and I finally got the adoption agency's approval. They said they would have a baby for us in six months. I can't work and raise a baby too, so that puts my job up for grabs. You're the logical person to take over. Now you floor me with this. Are you sure you know what you're doing? Six months, that's all I can give you. I'd like five with a firm commitment but I'll settle for the six."

"Lizzie, this will be my last chance to go for my doctorate. If your offer holds and I take the job, I could bring new focus to the position. You know I never do anything half way. Do you want an answer now?"

"I think you're capable of giving me an answer now. That's why I hired you in the first place. I've never regretted that choice, Dory, not once. You've proved yourself time and again. You're like me. You can make a decision and live with it. I have to know and I have to know now so I can start scouting for a replacement. Six months. You can finish that degree at Columbia, can't you? And, just so you don't get too wrapped up in this live-in relationship, I think you should consider doing some freelance work in the meantime. Take a look at this. It came down from on high today."

Dory scanned the printed words and then laughed. "You're one shrewd fox, Lizzie. That's called covering your tail, in this business."

"Look, Dory, I think I've known all along that you were planning this move. You're right. This might have come down from on high, but it was my idea. Who better than you to do a few profiles on eligible, handsome senators and congressmen? Pay's good too. Top dollar. A person could live a full year on what you'd make, say on just four of them. Quality, of course. Standout casual pics, that sort of thing. Say you'll take it so I can let my ulcer rest."

"Okay, but it means I'll have to work like hell."

"Dory, when do you plan to leave?"

"I'd like two weeks, but if you need three, I can handle

14

that. That should be more than enough time to break in Rachel Binder and Katy will be there to take up any slack. You do agree with Rachel as the logical choice, don't you?''

"No question about it. Two weeks it is. Will that give you time to sublet and handle all the mundane details of moving?''

"I can manage. Weekends I'll be going to D.C. to help Griff and find some place to live. Lizzie, I'm grateful, I truly am. I was hoping you'd be fair, but *generous* and fair is something I didn't count on.''

"Listen, I'm being selfish too. I might want to come back here some day and I don't want to burn any bridges. You're good, Dory, and there will be no qualms around here. I'll feel right turning it over to you if that's your choice. I want you to promise me something. I want you to call me in three months and tell me how it looks from where you're standing. You owe me that.''

"That's fine with me. I'm afraid I've been lax in not congratulating you on the adoption. I know how long you've waited for this. Jack must be delighted.''

Lizzie laughed as she toyed with a pencil. "He's got the room painted and decorated. He bought a rocking chair and is sanding it down. Supposedly, it's some kind of antique and hundreds of years old. Can you just see me in a house with antiques?''

Dory laughed as she looked around the starkly modern office. Chrome and glass were everywhere. "Give it time, you might learn to like it. I'm going to miss this place. You've all been good to me. It's hard to say good-by.''

"It is just temporary, isn't it, Dory?'' Lizzie asked in a pinched tone.

"I don't know. I'll call you in three months and that's a promise.''

"Here's our coffee. Put it here on the desk, Susy.''

Lizzie poured, then blew softly into her cup, watching Dory over the rim, her eyes full of unasked questions. "Damn it, I want to know more, Dory. Call it curiosity, concern or just plain nosiness. Somehow I didn't think you were the type for a live-in relationship. I'm not saying it's wrong. For me,

sitting where I am, it just doesn't compute. And going back
to school. That's a mind bender right there. Do you have any
idea of what size chunk you're biting off? You're leaving the
city and your job, you're going into a live-in relationship, and
you're going back to graduate school. It's a goddamn mind
bender is what it is. I always knew you had guts and if
anyone can do it, you can. I just hope that you've looked at
all sides of it. I don't want you to have regrets later. Consider
me a sister now and not your managing editor."

Dory leaned over the desk, her face earnest and sincere. "I
have thought about it. I have to admit I had some doubts. I
still have a few but I have to take a shot at it. I love Griff.
That's my bottom line. As for marriage, maybe I love him
too much to marry him right now. I never do things halfway,
you know that. And you know how important my doctorate is
to me. I can't keep putting it off forever. I'll give it my best
shot and go on from there."

Lizzie sipped at the hot coffee. "This stuff is mud. My
ulcer is going to complain. I like you, Dory, I always have.
Everyone here on the staff thinks highly of you. None of us
would stand in your way. Hell, what I'm trying to say is if for
some reason things don't work out, don't wait six months.
Saving face is not an American trait."

Dory smiled. "I'll remember that. It's nice to know the
door is open. But I can't make any promises."

"You're really sure you need that doctorate? How long
will it take?"

Dory flinched. She really didn't want to talk about going
back to school. Not now anyway. "I only have another year
to go. When I copped out that last year and came to work
here it was the right thing to do at the time. I'd had enough of
school and working part time. I cheated myself, I know that
now. I've always been sorry I never finished. I'll handle it."

Lizzie looked at her sharply but dropped the subject. "I
wish you the best, Dory. I hope things work out the way you
want them to. We'll keep in touch."

"Thanks, Lizzie, and my best to you too."

Lizzie stared for a long time at the chair where Dory had

been sitting. Blunt fingers with squared-off nails tapped at the smooth surface of her desk. The conversation ricocheted around her brain. The blunt fingers tapped faster. Suddenly the fingers stilled and a wide grin split her features. Her money was on Faraday.

Back in her own office Dory closed the door behind her. For some reason she felt cold and clammy. An interview, a conversation really, with Lizzie shouldn't be having this effect on her. Lizzie was on her side. What more could she want or expect? She slid into her chair and leaned her head back. Why was she feeling so light-headed? Taking a deep breath, she lowered her head to her knees. Another deep breath. Her mouth was dry, as if she'd eaten too much peanut butter. She didn't like what was happening to her. Was this some kind of warning? Surely it couldn't be an anxiety attack. Only people like her mother had anxiety attacks. Why would she have one? Things were going smoothly. Everything was falling into place. She almost had the world by the tail. Her breathing was almost regular now. Paper bags. People used paper bags when they hyperventilated. Was that what was happening to her? Was that the same thing as an anxiety attack? What did you do if you didn't have a paper bag? Exactly what she was doing. Nothing. A picture of herself carrying a brown grocery bag in her purse made her smile. "Just take the bag out of my purse and put it over my head." God, what if she had to say that to some stranger? Never! Get it together, Faraday, she told herself firmly. Pick up your head and wipe off your hands. Handle it. *Take control*. Don't *lose* control.

It was a good ten minutes before she felt normal. Now she leaned her head back and closed her eyes. Managing Editor. Jobs like that only came around once in a lifetime. It certainly was something to think about. It was also something to keep to herself for the time being. She wouldn't share it with Griff now, especially when he was just getting started in his new job. What a long way he had come from the days when he worked for the ASPCA. She wouldn't do or say anything that could put a blight or a shadow on his confidence or happiness.

For now, Griff had to come first. Would her successful career be as appealing if Griff were not in her life? Would a life with Griff but without a career for herself be appealing? She didn't know, wasn't sure. For now, she could have the best of both. She was a reasonably intelligent woman and she should be able to handle both the man in her life and her career. It was something she really wanted, to return to school and finish her degree. But was that really true? Or was she using school as an excuse to go with Griff? The thought bothered her. It was the perfect time and the perfect opportunity. But was she really ready to go back to the academic life? *Really* ready? She shrugged. It felt right and that would have to be good enough. If it proved to be the wrong decision, she would handle it. Griff seemed to sense how important her doctorate was to her. Could that have something to do with her decision to go back to school? *She didn't want to disappoint him.* He found it admirable for a woman to pursue education, and she believed it brought their relationship to a more equal level. He already had his degree in veterinary medicine; she would soon hold a doctorate in the humanities. No, she couldn't disappoint Griff. It had to be Griff and Dory. Equals.

By the end of the day news of Dory's plans had spread through the entire fifteenth floor. She knew this had been engineered by Lizzie who, by showing her approval, sanctioned all the good wishes and congratulations of Dory's colleagues. David Harlow, the editor of *Soiree*, stopped by to congratulate Dory and offered her drinks and dinner at Lutèce the following day. In essence, this was an open declaration that *Soiree* would always welcome Dory back with open arms.

Dory was overwhelmed by Harlow's offer. In her eight years at *Soiree* she had rarely been in the man's presence. Several wild and exhilarating Christmas parties and one summer picnic hardly counted. David Harlow was a commanding, dynamic man who generated office gossip concerning his private life. Two wives and twice as many mistresses were attributed to this rather short, nattily dressed man with the bruised circles under his eyes. Because of the authority and timbre in his voice a person forgot about the road map of veins in his cheeks and nose and the beginning of ponderous jowls.

"I'd like that, Mr. Harlow," said Dory, as she accepted his invitation. Although she wasn't eager to spend an evening with this man, she realized it would be inopportune to refuse. Especially for Lizzie's sake. Dory's replacing Lizzie as managing editor would require Harlow's blessing and now was as good a time as any to pave the way.

He didn't smile or brighten at her acceptance, nor did he ask her to call him David. One didn't call Mr. Harlow David. Ever.

Jewel-bright eyes flicked over Dory's attire; he seemed to register satisfaction. "Fine," he told her, his voice conspiratorially muted, "I'll stop by around seven tomorrow and we can catch a cab from here."

Dory sat quietly for a few moments considering the brief exchange of words. For some reason she felt vaguely disgruntled. Katy always said it would take an act of Congress to make the big guy step down to the fifteenth floor to chat with the underlings. Was her leaving and the offer of Lizzie's job equivalent to an act of Congress?

The late afternoon sun slanted into the spacious office, turning the plants into shimmering green jewels. Dory looked for dust motes but could see nothing but the band of light that seemed to laser through the wide window. She suddenly felt claustrophobic—as though she were trapped in a paperweight, the kind she had when she was a child that snowed tiny flakes when you turned it upside down. An overwhelming urge to talk to Griff washed over her. She drew in her breath, not understanding the feeling.

Katy bustled into the room, jarring Dory from her deep thoughts. She closed the door behind her and flopped down on the chair next to Dory's desk. With the door closed they could indulge in familiarity. "I'm impressed. So is everyone on the damn floor. God, do you have any idea of the stir you just created? By the weekend, according to rumor, you'll either be having a raging affair that's been going on for years or going off on a 'business trip' with Big Daddy Harlow. Lutèce, no less. Mr. Harlow's secretary told Lizzie's secretary who told Irma who told me. What do you have to say about that?'' Katy grinned.

"With a network like this who needs Ma Bell? I was as surprised as you are. I've only spoken to him once or twice and both times it was at a Christmas party. He's being nice. Don't give me problems, and for God's sake shut the girls up, will you? You know how I hate gossip.''

"I'll do my best but it's going to be a lost effort. Wouldn't you rather assign me to something else?'' Not waiting for a reply, Katy rushed on. "I was going to invite you over to the house for dinner, but I can't come close to Lutèce in decor or food. So enjoy. We'll get together before you leave. How did it all go today?'' Her question was serious and Dory, long used to Katy's moods and questions, fell into the called-upon role.

"Good. Lizzie really surprised me. It's going to take some getting used to, I can tell you that. It's a chance of a lifetime, but so is going for my doctorate. I won't deny that I have a lot of thinking to do. Did you know about the adoption and the offer?''

"I had an inkling. Lizzie's secretary spread the word that an adoption agency has been calling Lizzie for several months now. That was something no one wanted to discuss because if it didn't come through for Lizzie we would all have been devastated. You know how badly she wants a baby. And who but you is capable of stepping into her job?''

"They could have brought someone in from outside. I was stunned. I had no idea whatsoever. This has been a day to end all days.''

"The day isn't over. You still have dinner and the theatre, and then there's tomorrow—dinner with the big boss. You will tell me what it was like, won't you? I won't sleep a wink tomorrow night, worrying about you.''

"For heaven's sake, Katy, why would you worry about me having dinner with Mr. Harlow?''

Katy pursed her full lips till they resembled a rosebud.

"Because Mr. Harlow was just divorced and divorced men get lonely and for God's sake, Dory, do I have to tell you that men, important men like David Harlow, sometimes bring pressure to bear on lowly employees to get . . ."

"My sexual favors?" Dory laughed. "Don't worry. I'm sure it's nothing like that. This is strictly business, I can feel it in my bones."

"That's what Cassie Roland thought," Katy mumbled.

"Okay, who's Cassie Roland?"

"Cassie Roland is the girl in the publicity department." Her voice dropped to a whisper. "They say Harlow lured her back to the stacks after closing time and had her bloomers off in the wink of an eye."

"Katy, I'm surprised at you for repeating such gossip. Did they get caught?" She giggled.

"Why do you think he was just divorced? Where in hell have you been for the past eight years? Everyone knows you can't get a job in publicity unless you sleep with Harlow."

"I never pay attention to rumors like that," Dory said. "Where's Cassie Roland now? Did she get a promotion?"

Katy doubled over. "She sure did. She lives in the Dakota and is driving a Mercedes 380SL. She *says* she's doing freelance work."

Dory's stomach churned. "I'll handle it."

"Will you be going to D.C. this weekend?"

"I'm going to leave early Friday. Griff's partners' wives have been lining up apartments for us to look at. Griff will be staying with John for the time being. He hasn't even left yet, but I already miss him. Just knowing he won't be here in the city after tonight gets to me."

"And yet you say you aren't ready for marriage. I don't understand you, Dory. You're obviously crazy about the guy, yet you won't marry him. A live-in relationship could get sticky. You know, everyone isn't as liberal as we are. How much do you know about his partners' wives and the other women you're going to be associating with? Not much, right? I'd hate to see you get hurt, Dory, or dumped on, for that matter. I suppose you're sophisticated enough to handle it all, but is Griff? He seems like such a sweet guy, and he's going to be hanging out with some pretty influential people if he goes into equine medicine. You're talking about political clout, old money. Look, I'm talking to you like a mother, now. You can't just think about yourself—you have to think about Griff. Don't get so involved you can't walk away. I want to make sure that whatever you do you do for the right reasons.''

"It will be for the right reasons, believe me. I've been honest with Griff and he's been honest with me. He says he understands and will wait for me to make my mind up. I didn't jump into this. I've given it a lot of serious thought. For me now, at this point in time, this is my best move. I'll deal with later when later comes. All I know is I love him and I love my career. I have to find a way to combine the two of them, and going back for my doctorate is the first step. It's the best I can do for now. Everything is up front. Neither of us would have it any other way.''

"Okay, I can buy that,'' Katy said, sinking deeper into the leather chair. One shoe slipped off and she sighed with relief. "If I could just take off about twenty-five pounds, I know my feet wouldn't hurt so much.'' She grimaced. "How you manage to walk around in those three-inch heels is beyond me. What's the shoe count this month? I picked one hundred sixty-six in the pool. Just tell me if I'm close.''

Dory laughed. At first she had been less than amused when she found out the girls in the outer office were running a pool on her shoes. Then she had been flattered when they continued the practice. "No way. Pay your money and take your chances like everyone else.''

"Much as I'd like to chitchat some more, I have to clean up my desk, run down to copyediting, and then it's home for me and the love of my life. I'm referring now to my cat, Goliath, not my husband. We're not speaking. It was his turn to do the laundry last night and he copped out. He said his back hurt. He's starting to give me that 'women's work' routine. It isn't sitting too well with me.''

"That's because you make more money than he does. I

told you, every dollar you earn above his is a dollar's worth of power. Guess you're going to have to turn down your next raise. You're due next month, aren't you?'' Dory's voice was light, teasing, but there was something in her eyes that made Katy think twice before she answered.

"I would never turn it down. I would, however, do some serious reevaluation of my marriage."

Dory said nothing, but her eyes were sympathetic as she watched Katy bend over and struggle to slip her swollen foot into her espadrille. She winced and Dory looked away. "I'll see you in the morning and thanks again for the invitation."

"Any time," Katy said, limping from the office.

The end of another day. For some reason Dory felt saddened at the thought. There weren't too many days left. She couldn't start thinking wishy-washy thoughts now. The die was cast; she was leaving. Maybe she would return and maybe she wouldn't. For now she had an evening with her aunt and Griff to look forward to. His last night in town and he was generously offering to share it with her and her aunt. It pleased her that he was going to the theatre after a busy day and all the last-minute details that had to be taken care of before he could leave in the morning. That was so like Griff. He really put out for her in more ways than one. And, in her own way, she did the same thing. It was give and take. Griff wouldn't exactly 'suffer' through the play but she knew he would rather be doing something else. Thoughtful, kind, wonderful Griff.

Dory straightened her desk as she made her brief call to Griff to arrange their meeting in the coffee shop. He was agreeable as always. "Love you," Dory said softly.

"Yeaaaaaah," Griff drawled.

Dory knew when Pixie walked into the coffee shop, even though she couldn't see her. Pixie's entrance had created a hush. Dory smiled. There was no doubt about it. Pixie was an attention getter. She stood up and waved. "Over here, Pixie."

"My God, you look stunning, Dory. You do take after our

23

side of the family. I'm not late am I?'' she asked, looking
around. "Where's Grit? He is coming, isn't he?''

"Of course. He'll be here any minute now. Good Lord,
where ever did you get that outfit? Is that a new wig? Those
aren't real diamonds, are they? Is that cape really lined with
ermine?''

"One thing at a time. You wouldn't believe me if I told
you. Yes, the wig is new. I always wanted a black wig. I had
to take this one because all the others made me look like
Cher. I'm as skinny as she is but there the resemblance ends.
I had to glue it. There's a high wind out there. Of course
these diamonds are real. Your mother would give her eye
teeth for them. I needed a cape and this was the only one I
could find. What difference does the temperature make? The
theatre will be air-conditioned. You can wear ermine any
time, any place. What are we having to drink?''

"Coffee. Here comes yours.''

Pixie looked around to see if alcoholic beverages were
served. Seeing nothing but a coffee urn, she rummaged in her
bag and came up with a silver flask. She faked a sputtery kind
of cough and poured liberally for the waitress's benefit.
"Medicinal purposes.''

"If that's your story, it's okay with me,'' the waitress said
wearily.

"Smartass.'' Pixie grimaced.

Dory stifled a laugh. "Here's Griff.''

"You didn't tell me he was this good looking,'' said Pixie.
She held out her hand to Griff. "Be continental and pretend
you're kissing my hand. I do so love attention. Look at these
poor starved souls in here. This will be something for them to
talk about for days.''

Griff swallowed hard as Dory made the introductions.

"It's all right, young man. I usually have this effect on
people. Isn't that right, Dory?''

"Absolutely,'' Dory said.

"I always wanted to be a household word. You know,
famous, that kind of thing,'' Pixie said, yanking at the black
wig.

"In Mother's house you're a household word," Dory said as they sat down. "She called me today and told me you went for your annual checkup. How did it go?"

"The doctor was dumbfounded. He couldn't find anything wrong with me. Your mother seems to think I'm senile. I sent her a telegram saying I would live. That should ruin her day tomorrow when she gets it. The doctor was amazed when he took my history and found out I had had so much repair work done. He said it was astonishing that a woman would go under the knife so often and for so little results. He also told me I should get a cat or some other dumb animal for my twilight years. I let him know what I thought of that in quick order. Grit, would you like a belt of this?" Pixie held out her flask. Griff shrugged and took a swig.

"Jesus, what is that?" he croaked.

"Some people call it white lightning. Others call it shine. I have a whole barrel in my kitchen. It was a legacy from one of my husbands. Right now, I can't remember which one. But it will come to me."

"Those gloves are certainly elegant," Dory said, peering closely at her aunt's hands.

"I only wore them because my hands are smeared with Porcelana. I do hate those damn liver spots. No one really believes they're giant freckles except your mother," Pixie said fretfully. "Shouldn't we be leaving? It's not nice to walk in after the play starts."

"I guess so. Why so quiet, Griff?" Dory asked.

"No reason. Here, let me help you . . . Pixie." He looked wildly at Dory and mouthed the words. "What should I call her?"

"Of course you should call me Pixie. Everyone else does," Pixie said, craning her neck and knocking the wig off center. "Is it on straight, Grit ?"

"Looks all right to me. Dory?"

"Perfect."

With a swish of the ermine-lined cape Pixie sailed down the aisle.

Dory almost choked on her own laughter when Griff pinched her arm. "She's wearing Puma running sneakers."

"Guess her bunions are bothering her again. Don't worry, no one will notice unless she trips on that damn cape. Don't you just love her?"

Griff grinned from ear to ear as he linked arms with both women. "I'll be the envy of every man at the theatre. Not one but two beautiful women. What more could a guy ask for?"

"Not much," Pixie snapped. "I like him, Dory. He knows beauty when he sees it."

"There's one thing I hate about the theatre," Pixie whispered during the third act. "They don't sell anything for you to eat during the play. I like to nibble and sip."

Dory nudged Griff, who was dozing in his seat. She smiled. "He only came along because he knows I like the theatre. He'd rather be home watching a ball game. Isn't he wonderful, Pixie?"

"Do you go to ball games with him?" Pixie whispered.

"No, we go to wrestling matches. I hate them but I go and scream like everyone else. After I'm there I don't really mind. Griff loves wrestling."

"One of my favorite husbands loved wrestling but I can't remember which one. This play is boring. No wonder he went to sleep. Did I tell you about my pen pal?"

"No. Male or female? Ooops, sorry. What's he like?"

"Smashing. I think. We're really getting to know one another. One of these days I plan to meet him. He writes delightful letters."

"What kind do you write?"

"What do you think? I lie my head off. No woman ever tells a man the truth unless she's a fool. Women my age that is. You better wake your prince before the play is over. He might be embarrassed when the lights go on. He's a nice young man, Dory. I like him."

Dory let out a long sigh of relief. She had been waiting all evening for Pixie's opinion. Her two favorite people in the whole world and they liked one another. "I'm glad." Pixie knew how important her opinion was to Dory.

"I wasn't sleeping, merely resting my eyes," Griff said sheepishly. Pixie smirked. Plays were boring. She'd take the wrestling matches any day over Broadway.

"We'll put you in a cab, Pixie," Dory said. "I'd go along home with you but I have a big day tomorrow. And Griff has an even bigger one."

"You mean you and I aren't going for a nightcap? I thought we would go to Gallagher's and pick up some hunks and play around a little. Actually, I thought I would pick up a hunk and you could watch. Now that I met Grit I don't think you should play around. It doesn't hurt to look, though."

"Pixie, it's Griff, not Grit. Can I have a rain check? I know I'm missing out on hours of fun and I do love to watch you in action but I really do have a big day."

"You know me. Once I get a name in my mind it stays. To me he's always going to be Grit. Good name. Sturdy. Guts and all that. Of course you can have a rain check. Hang on to that guy, he's good stuff."

"I know," Dory laughed as Griff flagged down a cab and gave the driver the Dakota's address.

"Driver, ignore that address and take me to Gallagher's," said Pixie. "You know where it is, don't you."

"You bet." The driver grinned and winked at Pixie.

"Well don't just sit here, burn rubber, man," Pixie said, leaning back against the seat.

"You got it." The driver smiled to himself. He got them all. This night shift was something else.

It was really hard to say goodnight like this, but Dory and Griff had agreed to call it a night. They hailed separate cabs and Dory sank back against the cushions. She was too tired to care. What a day this had been!

Griff listened with one ear to the chattering cabbie on the ride across town. His thoughts were with Dory, her lovable eccentric aunt, and the move he was making in the morning. At this time tomorrow he would be in a new environment and loving every minute of it. His dream was finally coming true. And in a couple of weeks his dream would have a big gold ring around it when Dory joined him. It still bothered him that marriage wasn't in the picture, but he was coming to terms with the whole idea.

"What'ya say, buddy, am I right or wrong?"

"Hmmmmmnnn?" Griff said absentmindedly.

"That's what I say. If some crazy football team wants to give you five million smackers, take the money and run I say. Hell, the kid can always go back to school later on. Best goddamn running back I've ever seen. Heisman winner to boot."

"Hmmmmmnnn." The old lady was a pure delight. For some crazy reason she was everything he thought she would be. No wonder Dory was such a wonderful person. Imagine growing up with someone like Pixie. She had liked him, and approved, he could tell. And that flirty wink she gave him. He smiled to himself. She was okay in his book. But he cringed a little when he thought of his mother meeting Pixie.

The play wasn't bad, what he could remember of it. It wasn't that he minded going to the theatre or to a musical with Dory, but if he had a choice he would pick wrestling. Dory was a good sport about going with him, even though he knew she didn't particularly care for sports.

"I think Georgia can get along without him. Don't you think Walker is doing the right thing?"

"Hmmmmmnnn." Now that his big move was almost upon him he was more certain than ever that it was the right thing. The clinic had always felt right; it was the move with Dory that gave him jittery moments. He knew now it was right because it *felt* right, he told himself. And when he felt right it was all systems go.

"Driver, let me out here, I'm going to walk the rest of the way. Hell no, I'm going to run the rest of the way," Griff said, thrusting a ten dollar bill at the driver. "Keep the change and you're absolutely right about Walker, he is the best goddamn running back I've ever watched."

"You got it, buddy." The driver grinned as he pocketed

Griff's money. "See you around. Jersey is only across the river."

Running? Griff looked down at his evening clothes and his shiny shoes. Without a moment's hesitation he bent down and took off his shoes and socks. What the hell, it was only four blocks. No one in New York would give him a second thought as he raced by in his bare feet. Damn, he felt good. Tomorrow he was going to feel even better.

Chapter Two

Dory's stomach churned all the way down in the elevator as she stood beside David Harlow, feeling his shoulder brush insistently against her own. She had been aware of the speculating glances from the women in the outer offices as Mr. Harlow escorted her to the elevator. Word was out that he was taking her to dinner. She must have been mistaken, Dory cautioned herself; those same speculating glances couldn't have been touched with pity. Could they?

Mr. Harlow stood aside to allow her to walk through the revolving doors in the lobby. He walked too close and she resented the way he cupped her elbow in his hand as they walked to the corner.

"A taxi? Or would you rather walk?" Harlow asked.

"Let's walk. It's a nice evening. We could use the exercise after sitting in an office all day." There was no way she was going to sit in a taxi with David Harlow. If all the stories were true, and she was beginning to suspect they were, she had no intention of allowing him to paw at her.

They made small talk as they walked to the restaurant. She winced and tried to draw away from him when he put his arm around her shoulder as they waited to be seated. There was something possessive in his touch, something too deliberate, too firm, too certain.

"Drink?"

"Whiskey sour on the rocks," Dory replied smoothly. She

wouldn't allow him to rattle her. And she wouldn't have more than two drinks with this man. She needed her wits. This was supposed to be a spectacular day! A day that held such promise for her future . . . if she wanted it. She wouldn't allow a man like David Harlow to spoil it for her. Why hadn't she made some excuse that she couldn't join him for dinner? She should have. But she had been so filled with herself, so confident, and he had approached her at the height of her ego trip. All through the afternoon she had had time to reconsider, but by then it was too late.

"The food here is excellent," Harlow said as he lifted his drink to toast Dory. "Here's to a long and fruitful relationship."

"I'm leaving, Mr. Harlow. How long and fruitful our relationship will be still remains to be seen." Her mouth was dry and she could barely get the words out of her mouth. She didn't like this man. Neither his reputation as a lecherous bastard nor his arrogance.

"You'll be back," Harlow said loftily. "I carry a lot of weight at the magazine. I have your future right here in my hip pocket, Dory. You and I could make an excellent . . . working team." Dory was fully aware of the pregnant pause in his statement. "I personally approved of Lizzie's choice to have you succeed her. I've already gone to the board of directors and read off your qualifications like a litany. They were as impressed as I. We're all looking forward to your return."

"I haven't even left yet. And, I didn't say I would be back. I haven't decided." Dory didn't like the turn the conversation was taking. "Why all this sudden interest, Mr. Harlow? You've never expressed interest in my career before this."

"Darling, a man of my position cannot offer his attentions to every little copy girl whom *Soiree* employs. I admit I am irrevocably attracted to executive women who share my station and power. Didn't you know, I'm an equal opportunity employer!" Harlow seemed to find this extremely funny, and as he laughed he firmly gripped Dory's hand. "I could be of tremendous help to you, Dory. The right word here and there,

31

and you could make it all the way to the top. I could do that for you.''

Dory cringed and tried to cover her distaste, hating herself for her pretended politeness and her reluctance to make an enemy of this man. She knew she should simply stand, excuse herself and leave him. To hell with David Harlow. She didn't need this weasel . . . did she? Evidently, *he* thought she did. How slick he was. So certain she would seek his patronage. Dory forced what she hoped was a smile to her lips. ''Are you saying I won't be able to succeed without your help? What about those qualifications you litanized for the board?''

''Dory, I'm not quibbling about your ability. Your ideas have always been creative and valuable to the magazine. All I said was I could help you make it to the top. Success requires a particular type of woman. A sophisticated worldly woman who knows where her allegiances lie. I believe you're that kind of woman.''

''You didn't answer my question. What would I have to do to have you in my corner?'' Her heart was pumping madly and she was certain the man across from her could hear it.

Harlow set his drink down and leaned across the table. Dory felt herself shrink back into her chair. He reached for her hand again. Swallowing hard, she steeled herself against the feel of his clammy hands on hers. His flat white skin repelled her. Still, she didn't withdraw her hand. ''We're both mature, consenting adults,'' she heard him say. ''Don't play games with me. The only time I play games is in the bedroom. How good are *you* at games?''

''I manage,'' Dory said in a strangled voice. This couldn't be happening to her. She couldn't be sitting here, listening to this man threaten her integrity. She couldn't be letting him hold her hand. For what? For what, for God's sake? For a job? Was she actually compromising herself to this miserable excuse for a man? She had to do something, say something, get out of this somehow. ''There are other jobs.''

''Of course there are, my dear. This is New York. I think it's safe to say I know every editor-in-chief on every magazine in the city. I'm sure you could *apply* at any one of the magazines."

There it was, out in the open. She knew exactly what the words meant. If she didn't play ball, his way, she was out of a job and she wouldn't find it easy to get another one, not if he knew every editor-in-chief in the city. She could feel the bile rising in her throat. She withdrew her hand from his grasp and brought the glass to her lips. She gulped the sour drink and finished it in two swallows. She had to get out of here, back to her apartment. She would never come back to this sleazy city, with all its sleazebags like David Harlow. Griff. Think about Griff and a new life. She didn't have to sit here and listen to this weasel with his slick words and heavy threats. All she had to do was get up and walk out. Tell him to go to hell, drop dead, who did he think he was talking to anyway? This was sexual harassment at its worst. But if she did that, there would be gossip. Shameful things would be said. People would look at her and snicker. They'd talk about her behind her back. They'd say things and believe them, terrible, degrading things. Who would hire her with something like that hanging over her head? She had to do something, say something, get through this somehow.

"I'd like to order now. I have an early day tomorrow." After dinner she would make a graceful exit.

David Harlow leaned back in his chair and opened his menu. A smile played around his mouth. They were all alike. The woman hadn't been born who wouldn't climb in bed for the promise of money and some semblance of power. Words like *threat, coercion*, were not in David Harlow's vocabulary. This one was an easy piece. He wished he had noticed her earlier.

"May I suggest the lobster . . ."

Griff slid behind the wheel of the clinic van and stared at the ashtray full of plum pits. He grimaced. John's wife might look as if she'd stepped off a *Vogue* magazine cover, but she was the sloppiest woman he had ever come across. Tissues littered the floor and the stale scent of her perfume was

33

embedded in the velour seat covers. He hated it. Goddamn, the van was for clinic use, not for Sylvia to joyride around in. That Sylvia might consider him to be joyriding didn't enter his mind. He was picking up Dory at the airport and then they were going apartment hunting. There was a difference.

There were times when he felt boxed in, almost trapped. For the past several days the feeling had grown stronger and stronger, making him uneasy and skittish. He had hungered for this chance for so long, had worked so hard toward this end that he didn't understand his discomfort. It must be the practice. Surely it had nothing to do with Dory. Or did it? He loved her. God, how he loved her. Maybe it was Dory he was really worried about and not himself. After all, it was Dory who was giving up her career. It was Dory who would have to make a new life for herself here in the D.C. fishbowl. Dory would be starting from scratch. He at least had a job, colleagues he liked and admired, and a purpose in life. Was he robbing Dory of the very things he was gaining? Was he being fair to her, to himself? Hell, Dory was a vibrant, go-for-it young woman with sophisticated savvy. Wherever she went she would take those traits with her. Dory was Dory and that was why he loved her. So why was he uneasy?

He liked New York, even loved it, but when opportunity knocked he had to respond. Everyone had to respond to a dream at one time or another. This move was a must if he was to get on with life and career. He knew in his gut that another opportunity like this wouldn't come along again. The timing was perfect and Dory was part of the dream; she belonged in it. But was this what Dory really wanted? Was he being fair to her? She said he was, and he had to believe her. She said it was right, felt right. And, she had added, it was the perfect opportunity for her to finish her studies. In the end the decision had been hers.

Griff sighed. If all this was true, then why did he feel so anxious? Why was he so skittish? What was really bothering him?

The mere fact that anything at all was bothering him made him mad as hell. He hated it when he couldn't solve problems, come up with the right answer and get on with things. He was never one to sit and ponder. Either the dream was right or it wasn't. He loved Dory and Dory loved him. The practice was a golden opportunity, a step onward and upward for his career. He was happy with his decision to move here. If it was possible to be delirious with joy that Dory was moving here with him, then he was delirious with joy. So what was the problem?

The lack of commitment on Dory's part, perhaps? Her decision not to get married at this time? That's what it was. It was too loose. Not exactly temporary, just loose. When things were loose they could go either way. Marriage was a big step, an awesome responsibility. Perhaps Dory was right in not wanting to take such a step yet. Giving up her job, moving to a strange place, going back to school were probably all the decisions she could comfortably handle right now. He should understand it and he did understand it. He just didn't like it. He wanted to marry Dory. He wanted her to be the mother of his children. She wanted those same things, but she didn't want them right now. He was going to have to accept that because he loved her. He felt better now that he had put words to his feelings. The bottom line to his edginess was the lack of commitment. He could and would live with it. He had no other choice.

Christ, he was tired. He hadn't realized how tired he was until he saw Dory step off the plane from New York. All he wanted to do was take her in his arms and fall asleep against her softness. No thought of sex entered his mind. The clean fragrance of her was a balm to his senses. They kissed, a long, hungry kiss that made his head reel, oblivious to the stares and smiles of the other travelers. National Airport was a great place for kissing.

"Don't tell me the smell in this van is from some poodle, because I'd never believe it," Dory teased.

"John's wife was using it till their car was fixed. Needed new shock absorbers or something. She isn't the neatest person, as you'll find out. I didn't think you'd want to stay with them so I took a room at the Airport Holiday Inn.

What's your feeling on orange bedspreads and drapes? You don't mind, do you?''

"Mind? I adore the color orange. I love motels, if you go with them. Tell me, what prospects do you have lined up for us to see? Griff, you look tired. Are you sure you want to bother with apartment hunting today? I'll go alone and only bring you to the most likely ones.''

"I am tired, but I'll be all right. We're going to look together and that's settled. Sylvia and Lily really knocked themselves out lining up apartments. I hope one of them pans out. By the way, we're having dinner with the four of them. I wanted you all to myself, but the sooner you meet them the better we're all going to be. The girls are dying to meet you.''

Dory felt a little annoyed. What if she didn't like "the girls''? How would Griff react? How like a man to assume that just because he and John and Rick got on so well, she would get on equally well with their wives. She was tempted to put her annoyance into words but changed her mind. Griff had made it clear that he liked the two women. He would never understand if she didn't, so it was grin and bear it. She was probably worrying about nothing. Griff didn't include any undesirables among his friends. If Griff liked them, so would she. Think positive, she told herself.

"Hungry?'' Griff asked.

"No. They served a bagel with cream cheese on the plane along with a copy of the *Wall Street Journal*. How about you?''

"I had some coffee and toast. We'll have an early lunch. I thought we'd start on the Virginia side and work toward D.C. I'd like to avoid the city if possible. Traffic in the morning is a bitch. First stop Arlington.''

They spent the morning looking at cramped apartments with no closet space and outrageous rental fees. Dory vetoed all of them. The last apartment building was a complete disaster. Two of the three elevators had "out of order'' signs on them with messages tacked below in green crayon, making it clear what the tenants thought. The lobby tile was grimy and artificial plants were heavy with dust, making Dory sneeze. The rent for a studio was six hundred dollars and a bargain, the manageress said in a squeaky voice. She reeked of stale beer and garlic.

"We'll let you know," Griff said hurriedly, as he ushered Dory past a loathsome rubber plant and out a smeared glass doorway.

They both inhaled deeply and Dory laughed. "Griff, the main road we were on before we got to the second apartment, what was it called?"

Griff checked his map. "Jefferson Davis Highway. Why?"

"I saw some town houses that looked nice. Why don't we take a look."

Griff shrugged. "Okay, but I think those rentals are more than I can afford right now."

"I'd like to take a look. Really, Griff, what we've been looking at is barely big enough for you, much less me."

The Georgian-style town houses were set back from closely cropped boxwood hedges and wide borders of colorful flowers. Dory liked them immediately. She jabbed at the buzzer of the manager's office and waited. Griff rolled his eyes and whistled under his breath. Dory knew he was thinking the rent would be outrageous. Outrageous plus utilities. They were here, it wouldn't hurt to look.

Dory blinked at the man who opened the door. He was a jock of the first order. Skin-tight Jordache jeans, ankle-high boots with a shine that any Marine would envy. From the looks of his arms and chest he pumped iron when he wasn't out jocking. His navy blue shirt had a sprinkling of dandruff on the shoulders. "Call me Duke, everyone does," he said in a phony Texas twang that was one hundred percent Brooklyn.

Griff seemed mesmerized by Duke's attire, so Dory took the lead. "We'd like to take a look at one of the houses if you have a vacancy."

"Well, little lady, I just happen to have two. A congressional aide moved out the last of the month and the place was just renovated last week. Two stews are moving out this weekend. It's a duplicate of the aide's with a different color scheme. Want to take a look?''

''That's what we're here for, pardner,'' Griff drawled in annoyance. He hated macho jocks almost as much as he hated politicians. Shady and slick, the lot of them.

''Is there a lease?'' Dory asked.

''Two-year lease but it's not firm. We bend if you bend. Get my idea?'' he said, nudging Dory playfully on the shoulder.

''Yeah, we get it. We pay off and it goes into your pocket, right, pardner?'' Griff snapped.

''It's a mean, hard, cold world around here. This ain't the nation's capital for nothing.''

''You're right. This is Virginia, not Washington, D.C.,'' Griff said as he ushered Dory through the doorway.

The smell of fresh paint assailed their nostrils. The place was antiseptically clean. The dove-gray wall-to-wall carpeting had been shampooed, the windows sparkled, and the fireplace with its Italian marble facade was a dream to behold. Dory loved it immediately. The kitchen was yellow and green, and she mentally hung green checkered curtains and added a hanging fern. A braided rug and some wrought iron furniture would make it bright and cheerful. She loved it. The first-floor powder room was a soft plum color. She could decorate with blue, deeper plum or stark white. Upstairs, the master bedroom with fireplace made her draw in her breath. Griff did a double take as Dory walked into the huge bathroom, done in shades of beige and dark brown. A king-sized bed with a spread to match the lightning zigzag foil of the wallpaper would be perfect. Congressional aides certainly knew how to live. She knew that the wallpaper and carpeting were the aide's choices, not the management's.

''Where did the aide go?'' she asked bluntly.

''Georgetown,'' Duke said in a belligerent tone.

Griff smirked. ''How much is the rent?'' he demanded.

''Nine hundred a month. Management pays all utilities. Look around some and if you're interested, come over to the office. This place will be snapped up by Sunday, so decide now. We require a two-month security deposit.''

"Twerp," Griff snarled, as Duke left the room. "Dory, I can see you love this place and I don't blame you after what we've seen so far, but there's no way I can afford it now. Maybe next year."

Dory's face fell. "But, Griff, there are two of us. I'll help with the expenses. How much were you willing to pay? You haven't said."

"I didn't want to look at anything more than six hundred. How are you going to help? You'll be going to school, and I wouldn't want to dip into your securities. I can't afford this, Dory. I'm sorry."

"Griff, I'm going to be doing some freelance work for Lizzie. Profiles of congressmen and senators. The pay is adequate, believe me. I can carry my share. Please reconsider. Look at this fireplace. Can't you just see us making love in front of it on some cold, snowy night?" Not waiting for him to respond, she rushed on, "You're going to want to do some entertaining, and this place is perfect. We could even have a small barbecue in the back. Each house has a patch of garden in the rear, I saw it from the kitchen window. Some yellow canvas chairs and a table to match. Griff . . ."

"Honey, I didn't plan on you paying or helping out. If I can't afford you, then I have no business asking you to share my life. It's my responsibility to care for you."

"Just for now, Griff, until you get on your feet. Later we can change the arrangements if you want. Let me help. It's fair. With your furniture and mine this place could be a knockout."

"What about your apartment?"

"I'll sublet. No problem. Apartments on the Upper East Side are like gold. Say yes, Griff."

Griff stared down at Dory. She was probably right, but it hurt his ego that he would have to rely on her to pay half the rent. "Okay. I can see how badly you want this place. It's yours. Let's go talk to Superjock and settle it now."

"Oh, Griff, thank you." Dory threw her arms around his neck. "How far away is the Holiday Inn?"

39

"About four and one half minutes from this doorway," Griff laughed.

Twenty-seven hundred dollars poorer, Griff looked stunned when they left the rental office of the Clayton Square Complex. Dory was oblivious to his tight expression and tense shoulders. She had mentally decorated the entire town house, both floors, while Duke explained to Griff tiresome things like yard maintenance and the workings of the water heater and snow removal in the winter.

A fat, red-eyed pigeon wobbled. down the walkway in search of his dinner. Two more joined him in the quest, making Griff step off the walk onto the lawn that brashly displayed the mandate, "KEEP OFF THE GRASS."

On the short ride back to the motel Dory was eagerly anticipating the moment when she and Griff would be alone at last. It seemed months rather than days since he had left New York, and she had missed him dearly, especially that closeness they shared after lovemaking. Not since that first kiss at the airport had Griff attempted any intimacy with her. That sudden advance of hers in their newly rented town house didn't seem to count. That had been an impulsive move entirely her own and now, for the life of her, she couldn't remember if he had returned the gesture.

He's tired, poor dear, she excused him for his lack of ardor. Nevertheless, she was already looking ahead to the solitude of the motel room and Griff's embrace.

Immediately upon entering the room and locking the door behind him, Griff collapsed on the bed, one arm thrown over his eyes to block out the light from the wide windows. "Do you want to shower first, or shall I?" Dory asked, a bit annoyed. She assumed that Griff had missed her just as much as she had missed him, and when the door closed she waited for him to take her into his hungry embrace. Romantic, she accused herself. Give the guy a break. It's obvious he's worn out. Still, her charitable logic did nothing to lift her disappointment.

"You shower first, honey. I don't mind a steamy bathroom and used soap. Training from the Marines."

40

Dory sat down on the edge of the bed, her fingers ruffling through his dark wavy hair. "We could always shower together," she whispered invitingly, "that way, no one gets to use a steamy bathroom . . ."

Even before she uttered the words, she realized Griff was already asleep. He looked so pathetically weary, so vulnerable. Quietly, Dory closed the drapes to darken the room and then carefully removed Griff's shoes. She stripped off her dress and crawled onto the bed beside him, pulling up the spare blanket at the foot of the bed. Nestling down beside him, she offered her warmth and tenderness. In response to her, Griff turned on his side and wrapped her into his embrace, holding her.

Dory lay quietly. She wanted to talk about her plans for the town house. She wanted to talk about their new life and what living together would mean to both of them. Instead, she heard the deep, sonorous breathing that indicated he was sound asleep.

John and Sylvia Rossiter lived in a large white and wedgwood-blue colonial house set back from the street. Natives of Virginia, they had occupied the same house for twenty-three years of their twenty-four-year marriage. Griff liked and respected John Rossiter, and when he had made his offer three years ago, Griff had jumped at the opportunity. John had been in New York to read a paper on equine medicine, and the two had hit it off immediately and had been friends ever since.

While Griff liked and respected John, he always felt a little nonplussed about Sylvia. Sylvia was, as she put it, thirty-nine and holding. She admitted that she liked to be considered a trend setter in fashion and often attired herself in outlandish costumes that made Griff wince. Dory might recognize the style and the cost of Sylvia's wardrobe and be impressed, but secretly, he considered his partner's wife to be a plastic creation, and he often wondered how she managed to dress herself at all with those three-inch nails. He must ask Dory if she thought they were real. Sylvia couldn't cook or clean house, and John pretended to be amused by his wife's constant references to domestic chores, saying if God wanted her to be a domestic he would have permanently attached a mop to one hand and a broom to the other. The Rossiters' house had more than a lived-in look. Griff sought the right word and finally came up with "disaster." Satisfied, he rang the bell and grinned down at Dory. "This is going to be one hell of an experience for you. Just keep your cool and ride with it."

Sylvia Rossiter opened the door herself and smiled widely as she offered a carefully made-up cheek for Griff to kiss. Long, thin arms reached out to draw Dory to her but not before her eyes added up the prices of Dory's complete outfit, right down to the shoes. Outrageous lashes fluttered wildly as she calculated. She approved.

Dory fought the urge to sneeze at the cloying smell of Sylvia's perfume. Later, Griff told her it always reminded him of a cross between Pinesol and rose water.

"Darlings, darlings, darlings!" she cooed shrilly. "Come along, we're all shivering out on the patio. As you can see, I didn't get a chance to clean today, or yesterday or the day before that." Her tone indicated it was not something she *ever* planned on doing. "We'll just get a few drinks in you and you won't feel the chill. John is already cooking. Dory," she trilled, "I just know you're going to love it here, and you are not to worry your pretty little head for one minute about what people will say. If I hear so much as one word, I'll straighten it out immediately."

"She means it," Griff said. "She's hell on wheels about justice and the American way." It was Dory's turn to be nonplussed.

"That's a lovely outfit you're wearing," Dory said, smiling as she, too, mentally calculated the cost of Sylvia's outfit—the culottes with the tight band about the knee, raw silk in the palest shade of pink she had ever seen; a long, karate-style coat with a three-inch-wide crimson obi. Shoes to match the obi completed her outfit. It didn't go for a penny less than seven hundred dollars. Sylvia had four strands of jet-black beads at her throat and a matching band of beads and fringe worn low on her forehead. Dory felt awed, not so much at the cost but at the sheer audacity of the outfit.

"Darling, there is a story behind this getup. I had just bought it in Bergdorf's on my last trip to New York. There I was, carrying this outfit, walking down the street, minding my own business, wearing all my really good jewelry, when these four hoodlums started tracking me. I was more than a little nervous. I knew they were going to attack me any minute. Just any minute! I don't mind telling you I had to make one hell of a quick decision. It was either give up the outfit and jewelry or take a chance that someone might see me run into Ohrbach's. God!''

"As you can see, she opted for the unthinkable. She went into Ohrbach's," John Rossiter said, holding out his hand to Dory.

John Rossiter was a credit to his barber. His chalk-white hair and mustache were trimmed to perfection. His tailor had nimble fingers, as did the shoemaker who crafted his hand-made loafers. The family genetic pool could take credit for the weathered golden-brown skin that contrasted sharply with his prematurely white hair. His eyes were nut brown, observant, and keen, and the laugh lines etched deep grooves at the corners. Dory liked him immediately.

"Come along and meet Rick and Lily." Dory dutifully followed but not before she saw Sylvia roll her eyes at Griff.

Seated away from the smoke of the open barbecue, Lily Dayton was breast-feeding a cherub of a baby. Her husband sat beside her, his eyes glued to his firstborn son. Dory's first thought was, Madonna and Child. Griff had a strange look on his face as he watched the baby suck, making soft little sounds in the quiet of the patio. A spurt of grease shot in the air from the barbecue, startling Dory. She looked up; Sylvia stared pointedly at Lily and grimaced.

"Why you can't bottle-feed that child is something I'll never understand," Sylvia all but snapped. "She even does that in department stores," she said to Dory. Her tone became light and could almost be taken for teasing, but Dory knew better. She herself felt embarrassed for Lily, who was now propping the baby over her left shoulder, leaving her right breast exposed while she made him comfortable. "Disgusting," Sylvia hissed between clenched teeth.

Dory looked around. John and Griff, as well as Rick, seemed mesmerized by the large, swollen breast.

Rick, a tall, splinter-thin man, shook hands warmly. He reminded Dory of an intense young Anthony Perkins. A good surgeon, Griff had said. Sensitive hands, not a nerve in his body. Animals rarely had to be sedated while Rick examined them. "Welcome to our little group," Rick said softly. Everything about him seemed in place. He gave the impression that there was nowhere else he would rather be and that his life was in perfect order. It probably was, Dory thought, as her eyes went to Lily and the sleeping baby.

"Aren't you going to put him down now and button up?" Sylvia demanded.

"In a minute. I just want to hold him for a few minutes. It's a shock to their little systems to be taken from the warm breast and then placed in a cold bed."

"This is Dory, Griff's live-in," Sylvia said brashly.

"I'm so happy to meet you," Lily said. "I hope you can come over and lunch with me some time. I have some wonderful recipes I can share with you. Just ask Rick. I made a carrot cake that turned him into a beast."

Rick bared his teeth to show that he agreed. "We brought one with us. Sylvia never serves dessert."

"I'd like that," Dory lied. Imagine her swapping recipes with this little mother. Somehow Dory didn't think Lily would be interested in her recipe for Alabama Slammers. This child didn't look old enough to drink, and if she did, it was orange squash or grape Nehi.

The evening progressed and so did the chill. When it became apparent that everyone was shivering, Sylvia called a halt to the party. "I have a seven A.M. golfing date, kiddies, so we better call it a night."

Dory was thankful that the party was over. For the past two hours since finishing the burnt steak, she had been afraid to smile for fear tiny bits of charcoal would be stuck between her front teeth.

Lily's sweet voice continued chattering. "Have you been having a problem with the water, Sylvia? Ours is so hard I'm afraid to wash little Rick's clothes in it. I can't get the rust stains out of the toilet either. Do you know what I can use? It's really upsetting me."

The look on Sylvia's face was ludicrous. "I thought it was supposed to be like that." Dory turned her head to avoid laughing. Not for the world would she open her mouth and tell them her own secret for removing rust stains.

As they walked through the living room, Dory could hear Lily telling Sylvia that she had tried baking soda, vinegar and Clorox and nothing worked, and, "Sylvia, you might get germs if you don't do something."

"For Christ's sake, let's get the hell out of here," Griff said, sotto voce, as he led Dory out the front door. "See you Monday," he called over his shoulder.

"Well, what do you think?" Griff asked anxiously as he started up the van.

"They all seem very nice," she replied in a noncommittal voice. She had to think about the lot of them before she made any statements that she might regret later on. Slow and easy for now.

Griff laughed. "When you get to know them, they don't get better, they stay the same. John is fantastic, as you know. Sylvia is Sylvia. She's into clothes. Spending money is her hobby. She plays golf and tennis and drinks more than she should. She can't cook worth a damn and you saw how she cleans house. She does get a cleaning crew, or wrecking crew, to come in twice a year to give the place a once over and then she throws a party that would knock your eyes out. She's generous and friendly. You'll get along. Fashion is something you have in common."

Dory bit her tongue to keep from replying. She could see little that she and Sylvia Rossiter had in common, particularly in matters of taste.

"Lily Dayton is a lovely, sweet person, as you must have

45

seen." Dory wondered if Griff was aware of how his voice changed when he spoke of Lily Dayton. "She's wrapped up in her baby and so's Rick. They really and totally live for one another. She loves to bake and cook and fuss in the house. She had a garden this summer that was mind boggling. Rick said she canned vegetables and fruits for weeks on end. She has a cold closet in the basement where she keeps all the things she cans. It's remarkable," he said in an approving voice. "Rick said she knitted all the baby's blankets and sweaters last winter. Their house, while not as large and expensive as the Rossiters', is a showpiece. Lily refinished all the furniture herself, hooked the rugs, sanded down the woodwork, and repainted it. She has some priceless antiques that she's collected since she and Rick got married. I'll bet she can help you when you start decorating our place."

Our place. How wonderful it sounded. But he was wrong. Lily Dayton would have no part in her decorations. This was something she was going to do on her own. Imperceptibly, she moved a little closer to the door. She was annoyed. Did he have to be so damn complimentary where Lily Dayton was concerned? It surprised her and rankled that Griff had never even alluded to the fact that he admired homemaking. And babies. Maybe it was the baby that made him so agreeable and . . . just what the hell was it, she wondered. Was she jealous? Of course she was jealous. She wanted Griff to look at her the way he looked at Lily. She wanted to hear that approving tone in his voice when he spoke about her and her accomplishments. She inched still closer to the door. What could he say after he said, "Dory works for *Soiree* magazine in New York." Now he could say she was going for her doctorate. Big deal. She suddenly realized she would never get that reverent approval unless she singlehandedly canned eighty-seven quarts of string beans. Men! She didn't think she was going to like Lily Dayton.

"By the way. You were a knockout. Everyone liked you. Sylvia will be after you to find out where you get your clothes. You looked every inch New York and Fifth Avenue. New dress, huh?"

"Not really. It's three days old." Dory grinned. It was okay now. Now he noticed her and was paying her compliments. There for a minute she had felt like the forgotten woman. He approved of her and the way she dressed. He approved of her.

"When do your classes start?"

"I thought I'd come down early next Friday for final registration. I have Katy doing all the paper work and making the phone calls. I don't anticipate any problems."

"Are you sure you're going to be able to handle the freelance work and school, not to mention the house?"

There it was again. Keeping house. Homemaking. Was that what he wanted? A Homemaker?

"Of course I can handle it. We're just two people, so how much housekeeping can there be? You aren't messy and neither am I. If we both pick up after ourselves, there shouldn't be much of a problem. If I must, I can engage a cleaning person once a week. I don't want you to start worrying about me and how I'm going to cope. You have enough on your mind without all of this. Let me handle this end of it, Griff." Even to her own ears she sounded so certain, so confident. But was she? If she were back in New York, at *Soiree*, among people she knew and places that were familiar, her confidence would be well founded. Here in Washington, everything was new—new people, new situations, the pressures of school, making a home for herself and for Griff . . . why, she didn't even know where the grocery market was or where to get a really fine cut of steak. Dry cleaners . . . Dory gulped back a wave of doubt. She would handle it, she must handle it. Smiling, she decided to cross those bridges when she came to them. For now, she'd concentrate on Griff. "What do you say we get back to that motel where we can be alone. Together?"

"She's a mind reader, too," Griff grinned in the darkness. "I really dislike bucket seats in automobiles. Wiggle closer, we can at least hold hands."

Dory reached for his hand and gave a little involuntary shiver. "Cold?" Griff asked. "The evenings always get damp

47

this time of year, even here in Virginia. Autumn is hard upon us, gal, it's already the middle of September, or almost. Only seventeen shopping weeks till Christmas. Think you can handle it?''

Dory laughed. ''Goon. Reminding me about Christmas when I'm still in the midst of setting up a home for us. And school . . .'' Her tone softened, becoming a little breathless. ''Christmas. Our first Christmas, Griff!''

''Home. Our first home, Dory,'' he mimicked her dreamy tone, teasing her. Then more seriously, ''Would you mind if I invited my mother for at least a part of the Christmas festivities?''

''Not a bit. If you think she'd come . . .''

''Mom doesn't set herself up as a judge, Dory. You should know that. Mom would love to share the holidays with us.''

''As long as you're talking family, I have this zany aunt who actually advocates the racier side of life . . .''

''It's settled then.'' Griff squeezed her hand. ''We'll invite Pixie, too!''

Dory settled back against the seat, still holding fast to Griff's hand, resting it on the top of his thigh, feeling the roll of the muscles as he manipulated the gas pedal and the brake. It was nice to know that he was thinking ahead to Christmas and the holidays and that she was first and foremost in his plans. There would be a continuity to their lives, a kind of settling down, a comforting safeness. With Griff, she knew exactly where she would be for Christmas and exactly what she would be doing. No more jaunting off for winter holidays at the Christmas season. No more touring around the ski slopes or lying in the Bahama sun with others who also lacked a connection and permanency in their lives. With Griff she had gained a definition of time and place. In December, at the holidays, she would be here, with the man she loved, in their very own home. If the excitement of spontaneous, last-minute plans was a thing of the past, that was all to the good . . wasn't it?

When Griff and Dory closed the door to their motel room, he took her into his embrace, biting lightly on the tender flesh beneath her ear. Dory heard herself laughing, delighted that Griff was once again the attentive lover he had always been. His hands impatiently moved to the tiny buttons at the back of her dress, hastily working the fastening, eager to bare the creamy skin of her shoulders and breasts.

Lips caressing, tongues touching, they stripped away the offending garments, exploring and kissing as though they had never made love before.

Dory's hands were hot and demanding, covering his flesh with eager deliberation. "Easy, love," Griff whispered in her ear. "We've got the rest of the night and I intend to spend every minute of it making love to you." His lips were pressed against her throat, his voice sending little tremors through her body. "Easy, love, easy."

In a graceful, swift movement, he lifted her into his arms and carried her to the bed, holding her against him while he threw back the spread and laid her gently down on the smooth sheets.

He stood beside her for a long moment, drinking in the long, sweeping lines of her body, traveling up the length of her slim thighs to the perfection of her small but sweetly molded breasts. The fire in his loins rose to his head, making him feel heady, knowing a deep, aching longing for her. She held out her arms to him, and with a sound that was close to a groan, he lay down beside her, entwining himself around her, drawing her close against him.

Dory's head was swimming with anticipation. Her body was ready for him, arching, needing, eager for his touch and for his ultimate possession of her. But he would not take her quickly, she knew; his would be a slow, artful exploration, giving, taking, claiming for his own. And when she would feel herself splitting into fragments, incomplete without him deep inside her, only then would he take her, filling her world and joining her to himself.

Their mouths touched, teasing little tastes of his tongue, while he held her so tightly that each breath was a labor. He anchored her body to his while her senses took flight, soaring high overhead until her thinking became disjointed, and her world was focused only on those places which were covered by his hands, by his lips.

Taking his dark head in her hands, she cradled his face, kissing his mouth, his chin, the creases between his brows. His mustache tickled and aroused, adding further sensation to the contact between their mouths, making his lips seem softer and warmer in contrast.

"Love me, Griff, love me," she implored, her voice deep, throaty, almost a primal cry of desire. The sound in the silent room made his passions flare. He covered her with his body, holding her fast with his muscular thighs, while he skillfully caressed her heated flesh. She drew his head down to her breasts, offering them. His lips closed over one pouting crest and then the other, nibbling, teasing, drawing tight loving circles with his tongue. His excursions traveled downward to the flatness of her belly and the soft, darker recesses between her legs.

Dory felt herself arch instinctively against his mouth, her head rolling back and forth on the pillow as though to deny the exquisite demand of her sensuality. Her fingers curled in his thick, dark hair, her body moved of its own volition against the caress he excited against her. Release, when it came, was the ebbing of the flood tide, seeping from her limbs and the sudden exhaling of her breath. She was floating, drifting on a cloud, the whole of her world consisting of his lips and her flesh and the contact between them.

Still, his movements were slow, deliberate and unhurried, although there was a roaring in his ears that was echoed in the pulses of his loins. His hands grasped her hips, lifting her, drawing her against him, filling her with his bigness, knowing his own needs now and demanding they be met. His breathing was ragged, his chest heaving as though he had run a mile. Lips met, lingered, tasted and met again. He moved within her imprisoning flesh, insistently, rhythmically, bringing her with him to another plateau so different from the first yet just as exciting. He rocked against her, feeling the resistance she offered, knowing that as she tightened around him as though to expel him from her, she was coming ever nearer to that climaxing sunburst where he would find his own consolation.

Panting, Griff's body covered hers, calming her shudders and comforting her until their spasms passed. It was with reluctance that he withdrew from her and silently pulled the covers over them, taking her in his arms to cradle her lovingly. Contentedly, Dory rested against him, sweeping her hand down the length of his body and finding him moist from her own wetness. Curled together in a dream of their own, they murmured love words until at last they slept.

Chapter Three

THE DAYS MOVED SWIFTLY BUT NOT SWIFTLY ENOUGH TO SUIT Dory. She concentrated on one thought: get to Virginia as soon as possible and be with Griff. She went through the motions at *Soiree*, but at the end of the day she wasn't certain she had accomplished anything. Her thoughts were on furniture, dishes, and lamps. Green plants and drapery fabrics were a close second. Her doctorate was almost an afterthought.

She packed with feverish intensity in the early hours of every morning. Boxes of books and her personal things would go with her in Griff's station wagon when she bade her final adieu to the Big Apple. Subletting the apartment had been no problem. Katy's cousin's boyfriend's sister was delighted to take it off her hands at a hundred dollars more a month than she was paying. An extra hundred to decorate with, Dory chortled to herself, and then later, that hundred dollars every month would buy what she wanted. Shoes, new blouse, lacy underthings. Whatever.

Never more than a cursory cook, she now mentally planned nourishing menus that she would serve on just the right dishes with just the right place mats and real napkins that had to be ironed. She would make a centerpiece and an exquisite dessert. She would need cookbooks. Katy could take care of that for her with a phone call to her friends in the publishing houses. Dory could imagine herself poring over cookbooks in front of the fireplace while Griff studied his veterinary journals.

Togetherness. Wonderful. Griff would sigh with delight and pat his stomach and look at her the way he looked at Lily Dayton. Homemaking would have its own brand of rewards. Candlelight. Dinner would always be by candlelight. She would make sure the atmosphere stayed romantic so Griff would have no cause to regret his decision to rent the town house. In the spring she would plant some pansies and tulips. Griff loved flowers and bright colors. Pots and pots of flowers. Maybe a few geraniums. Spring? Spring would be March. April. Six months away. Her stomach churned as she thought of the deadline she had promised Lizzie. She could play house for six months and get it out of her system, as Lizzie put it. Or she could settle in, marry Griff, and finish her doctorate. Or she could come back to *Soiree* and take on David Harlow and all the problems that would go with the job. Six months was a long way off. For now she couldn't think past Thanksgiving and Christmas. She would make it memorable for both Griff and herself. It would be their first Christmas. God, how she could decorate that place for the holidays. Just last year *Soiree* had done an in-depth interview on a wealthy woman who hand-made Christmas decorations for the Fifth Avenue crowd. They had been exquisite and the prices had been mind bending. Somewhere in the bowels of the *Soiree* building were cartons of those decorations that she herself had packed up to be stored. She vaguely recalled the wealthy woman saying she could have them for the wonderful job she had done on the layout. Feeling guilty because all the office girls wanted them, she had packed them up and then forgotten about them. Now, she would add them to the boxes to be transported to Virginia in the station wagon.

Dory fixed herself a cup of coffee and walked to the window. She certainly hoped she would sleep better once she was in Virginia. The past days, with only three or four hours of broken sleep, were doing nothing for her already impatient disposition. She wanted to be gone, to be with Griff in their new home. New home. How wonderful it sounded. How happy. A nice, warm, snug, safe place of their own. Decorated by her for Griff with loving hands. Griff couldn't help but approve. They were going to be *so-o-o-o* happy.

The heavy drapes swished open. To the east the sky began to grow light. A streak of orange-gold appeared on the horizon, dividing the space into two endless halves of smog and pollution.

The phone shrilled just as Dory finished making a second cup of coffee. She balanced the cup in one hand and cradled the receiver next to her ear. The voice on the other end of the phone delighted her. A wide grin stretched across her face as she carefully set the cup on the counter. "Pix! Talk about timing. I was just thinking about you. How are you?"

"Do you want the truth or an outrageous lie?"

"I'll take the truth. How's things in the Dakota where all the fancy people live?"

"B-o-r-i-n-g. But, yesterday I saw Yoo Hoo in the elevator. You know the one who wears the sun glasses and was married to that rock singer. Anyway, she took off her glasses when she saw me."

"You probably dazzled her with one of your costumes. What were you wearing and how many diamonds did you have on? By the way, where are you?"

"In the coffee shop downstairs. I thought I'd stop by to see you for a few minutes. Do you have the time?"

"Pix, for you I'll make time. Have you had breakfast?"

"Breakfast! Good God, Dory, if I ate breakfast it would kill me. I feel in the mood for Irish coffee and a bagel. Can you swing it?"

"Absolutely. I'll have it ready when you get here."

Dory opened the door at the sound of the buzzer. She stood back to view her aging aunt. For some reason she was always reminded of a rainbow when she saw Pixie. They hugged each other and giggled like two schoolgirls. "God, I'm exhausted," Pixie said, slumping down on the sofa. "It's a jungle out there in the morning."

"Tell me about it. I have to hack my way through it every day. What are you doing up so early? I thought you slept till three."

Pixie snorted as she gulped at her Irish coffee. "If you would just figure out a way to get your mother off my back so I can get on mine I could sleep till three. Ten days of celibacy is all I can handle."

Dory laughed. "Mom's at it again, huh?"

"I swear that woman has a private detective trailing me. I think I shook him this morning, though. She said I was becoming an embarrassment to her and she wasn't going to tolerate it anymore. Can you believe that?" Pixie snorted again as she straightened her silvery wig of cascading curls. "I think you put too much coffee in this cup. This is the way your mother serves it to the minister when he stops by to console her over my antics as she calls them. How do you stand her? I know she's my sister and your mother but she's missing out on all that life has to offer. She must spend at least twenty-one hours of every day worrying about what I'm going to do next."

"Well, what are you going to do?" Dory giggled.

"I already did it," Pixie said, filling her coffee cup a third time. "I put myself in the hands of the best plastic surgeon in the country and told him not to stint. You're looking at the results."

Dory frowned. "What did you have done?" She hated asking the question but she had to know. A sucker was born every minute. Not Pixie. Pixie wouldn't . . . or would she?

"I knew you were going to ask that. Not a whole hell of a lot. I got a boob job and a derriere lift. Doctor Torian, who by the way is a handsome devil, and a class act, said he was a skilled surgeon and not a miracle worker. My fanny is now featuring a silicone implant. It's so marvelous, I can't tell you. I can bounce like a rubber ball. I am disappointed in my boobs, though. I would have had a complete overhaul but the doctor said there was only so much he could do. So, I settled for this. But," she said, wagging a bony finger at Dory, "I know that when I walk away from someone I juggle. I mean jiggle. It was worth it," she grinned as she slurped the last of her coffee. "You used instant coffee, didn't you?"

"I'm impressed," Dory said in a hushed voice.

"So was your mother, that's why she has this detective on me. She says she wants me to be respectable. Can you believe that? What business is it of hers if I have my ass lifted?"

Dory watched in stunned amazement as Pixie literally leaped from the sofa. "See what I mean, I sort of bounce."

"You know Mom. She's . . . well, she's . . . what she is . . ."

"Dead from the neck down. I'll say it for you. You know I love her but she drives me nuts. I'm so horny right now I could scream. I don't dare do a thing with this cretin she hired to watch me. She had the gall to tell me that sex should be curtailed at fifty. Fifty!" Pixie screeched. "I could hardly believe my ears. Fifty! I sent your father a condolence card." Dory nearly choked on her coffee as she watched Pixie strut around the room. "I refuse, I absolutely refuse to be a geriatric casualty. You should do an article on the subject for that magazine you work for."

Dory's eyes grew thoughtful. "Pix, would you defy Mom and do a layout, baring all? Verbally I mean," she said hastily as she noticed a wicked gleam in her aunt's eyes.

"I thought you'd never ask," Pixie said, flopping down and then bouncing on the sofa. "Of course. Will it be in good taste? Even if it isn't, I don't care."

"Listen, Pix, if you're serious, I'll speak to Katy about it. If it can be done in good taste, you're our gal."

Pixie bounced up again and tugged at her wool sweater. "The talk-show circuit, residuals, commercials—will I get it all?"

"I wouldn't be surprised. Who's going to tell Mom?"

"He is," Pixie said, pointing to a man lounging next to a car on the street below. "I refuse to be a party to your mother's next anxiety attack. Aren't you going to be late for work?"

"I sure am. I have to get moving. Why don't you stay and finish off the coffee. Lock up when you leave."

"Would you mind if I stayed the better part of the day?

I could do some entertaining while I'm here. I have this friend . . ."

Dory turned to hide her smile.

The talk-show circuit yet! Hot damn, it might be good for a story at that. There must be a lot of older women who have the same feelings Pixie has. What do they do? How do they handle it? Her mind started racing as she pictured the layout and the intimate shots they could do of Pixie. By God, it would be interesting! *Soiree*'s readership, if you believed the last poll, consisted of twenty percent over the age of fifty-five.

All the way to the office her mind clicked like a computer. It wasn't until midmorning that she realized she hadn't thought of Griff or the town house once. She sat down with a thump. She was giving it all up. Permanently or temporarily. Damn, Pixie would make a terrific story, and with the two of them working together it would have been super terrific. She sighed heavily. Someone else could handle it. Someone else *would* handle it. She would have to read about it like everyone else from now on.

Katy's eyes bugged out when Dory presented her idea. She jotted down Pixie's address and phone number. By the time Dory left the conference room the entire floor was buzzing with the news that David Harlow himself had given the okay to do a cover story with Dory's sexy old aunt. They were even toying with the idea of putting Pixie's picture on the cover, Katy said.

"Harlow said you were to be commended," Katy gasped. "Commended, mind you. Not congratulated, but commended. Jesus, Dory, do you know who you have to be to get your picture on the cover of *Soiree* magazine?"

Dory giggled. "You can't say I'm leaving quietly. Fanfare, style, that's my departing theme. You'll all remember me in the days to come. Why don't you get us some lunch and I'll tell you how I'm going to decorate the spare bedroom."

"Again? You told me that yesterday and the day before."

"That was the living room. This is Griff's den. The extra bedroom is going to be his study. I thought all earth tones with a few splashes of color."

"Where are you going to do *your* work, *your* studying?" Katy asked.

For a moment Dory looked blank. "Oh, I suppose I could use Griff's desk or the kitchen table. It doesn't make a lot of difference where I study. I'm adaptable."

"I can see that," Katy said sourly. Her eyes narrowed as she stared at Dory. "It's . . . it's . . . commendable what you're doing. Don't slack off before you start." Her tone was sour and Dory picked up on it immediately.

"It's just that I have so much on my mind. How could I slack off. That's the main reason for the move. Don't worry. When you see me next, I'll be on my way. Do you think you'll have any difficulty calling me Doctor Faraday?"

"Not a bit. By the way, I left a pile of information on your desk and all the cookbooks are stacked in boxes. One of the stock boys said he'd drop them off at your apartment after work. There's even one on microwave cooking."

"Katy, that's fantastic. I'll buy a microwave. It will make things easy for me when I start school. Thanks for mentioning it."

The going-away party for Dory was held in the office at three o'clock. There was champagne punch in plastic glasses and assorted canapés, made by the girls, on paper plates. A Halston leather briefcase was her going-away gift from the office staff. Lizzie and Katy had chipped in and added a matching overnight bag. David Harlow handed her an envelope she didn't have the nerve to open. His eyes were too readable, too knowing. Suddenly, she felt as though she were swimming upstream in shallow water.

Later, after all the hugs and kisses, Dory walked through the offices for the last time and opened the envelope. A pink check (why were they always pink?) in the amount of one thousand dollars made her blink. Bribe was the word that came to mind. And then a second: pimp. She swallowed hard. She didn't want the check. She stuffed it and the envelope into her bag; she'd think of it as a microwave oven. A microwave and three pairs of shoes. Or six pairs of shoes

and an electric toaster oven. Or a new outfit and some school
books. Or, put it in the bank and let it grow some interest. Or
tear it up and forget about it? She disliked David Harlow
intensely. He was slick, unctuous. Hell, it was company
money, not David Harlow's personal money. That made a
difference. It didn't matter what she did with it. Tomorrow,
when she drove down to Virginia, things would look different.
One more day and she would be with Griff. Not even one
whole day. If she started early in the morning, as she planned,
she would be with him around noon. Perhaps they could even
have lunch if he was free. She ached for him. Her eyes
thirsted for the sight of him and her mouth hungered for his.
It was just hours now. Hours till he took her in his arms and
wiped away all thoughts of David Harlow and New York.

The Big Apple. She was actually leaving New York. In her
wildest dreams she had never imagined living anywhere else.
This was her city, her town, her people. Pixie lived here. Her
parents lived here. Her job was here. Wrong . . . Her job
used to be here. She didn't have a job anymore. Now she was
a free spirit. Her feelings were so mixed that she wanted to
cry.

As Pixie would say, this was fish-or-cut-bait time. All the
decisions were made. Now all she had to do was follow
through. She wasn't giving up her career entirely. She would
be keeping her hand in, in a limited way. Freelance work
would keep her active. School would definitely be an asset to
her later. Perhaps a doctorate wouldn't actually help her
career, but Ph.D. after a name never hurt. Doctor Dory
Faraday sounded good no matter how you looked at it. The
opportunity was here so why shouldn't she take advantage of
it? Everything would fall into place once she settled into her
new home. She could handle it all. She worked best under
pressure, when things were at sixes and sevens. Long hours
and rigid schedules had never frightened her. She could handle anything as long as Griff was in the picture. Anything.

Was she making a mistake by leaving the door open at
Soiree? Shouldn't she have cut the cord completely? If she

FERN MICHAELS

had resigned she wouldn't have anything to come back to if
things soured between her and Griff. God, why did she have
to think of something like that? She couldn't go off with
negative thoughts to start a new life. She had to consider the
temporary leave and the open door at *Soiree* as an option. An
option she could either renew or cast aside. It would be her
choice.

Damn it, she hadn't realized it was going to be so hard to
leave. Her life was here. This was life. Dear God, don't let
me be making a mistake, she prayed silently. No, it was the
right thing to do. Griff was the right thing. She loved Griff.
Happiness was being with Griff. A job was only a job.

A devil perched on her shoulder. If that's true, why aren't
you marrying Griff? Why aren't you making it for life instead
of this . . . whatever it is you're calling it in your mind?
"Shut up," Dory said tartly as she shrugged her shoulders,
hoping to dislodge the devil's unwanted voice that always
irritated her when she was in turmoil.

It was time to leave. She *was* doing the right thing. It felt
right and that would have to be good enough. Griff *was* right
for her. All the rest didn't matter. Not really.

Dory said her last good-by to Sara, her next-door neighbor,
promising to keep in touch. Sara handed her a thermos,
saying she knew Dory would want to get to Virginia as soon
as possible and not have to stop. Dory thanked her and was
off, the station wagon loaded to the top, the rear end notice-
ably lower than the front. Books were heavy. Thank God
Griff had flown to Washington and left the station wagon for
her.

Shortly after nine o'clock Dory uncorked the thermos and
took a healthy swallow. She turned on the radio. Someone
was shrieking about a love that lasts forever and ever and ever
and then some. She switched the station and Willie Nelson
warbled to life. She grinned. Griff loved the seedy, rambunc-
tious Willie with a passion. He had every tape and record the
man ever made and could sit and listen dreamily for hours on
end. He said Willie was better than any tranquilizer for his

60

animals and would probably make sure that his music was piped into the new clinic.

At eleven-thirty Dory guided the loaded station wagon into her assigned parking space. Sylvia and Lily, pushing a stroller, walked around to the parking area with Duke, the manager, walking just a shade too close to Sylvia. Lily smiled happily and hugged Dory. God, Dory thought, eleven-thirty in the morning and Sylvia looked as if she had spent the entire morning in bed. There was no mistaking the look on her face. Dory wondered if John was responsible for the contented, rapturous look—or could it be Duke? She couldn't help wondering. "How long have you been here?" she asked.

"Darling, for hours. The phone people were here at eight. They hooked up the washer and dryer at nine-thirty and the movers called to say they'd be here at two o'clock. Your refrigerator came a while ago and it's plugged in and running."

Dory looked pointedly at Lily. "No, I'm a slouch," she said. "I just got here. Little Rick naps in the morning. I had to bathe him and feed him and then he was hungry again. I haven't done a thing. But I'm here now and I'll be glad to do my share if little Rick can behave himself."

Duke smirked as he swaggered over to the car and offered to help with the heavy cartons. "Did you ever see such muscles?" Sylvia whispered.

"Can't say that I have," Dory said, bending over to take a box out of the car.

"I brought coffee and Lily brought some of her homemade blueberry muffins," Sylvia volunteered.

"Where's Griff?" Dory demanded. "Why isn't he here?"

"Darling, he's in McLean checking on some senator's horses. John went with him. You won't see him till late tonight or maybe tomorrow if they have to stay over. This is a whole new ball game for you, so you'd better adjust, darling." It was clear that *she* had indeed adjusted. Dory wondered if John had any idea how well.

"You'll get used to it, Dory," Lily said softly. "If you had a bundle of love like little Rick, you'd hardly notice Griff's absence."

Dory's heart plummeted. She had been looking forward to seeing Griff, and now if what Sylvia said was true, she might not see him till tomorrow. She would have to spend her first night in the town house alone. There would be no one to carry her over the threshhold. Griff would have carried her over it, she was sure of it. He was romantic in so many ways. "Damn," she muttered. Lily's eyes flew to the baby to see if he had heard. She frowned to show her disapproval. Dory winced and made a note to be careful of her vocabulary from now on.

"Why don't we have those muffins so we can all gain five pounds? Lily uses pure butter, tons of it," Sylvia complained. "Maybe Duke will be good enough to let us heat the coffee in his apartment. You don't have any pots. I'll do it. You two go along and I'll bring the coffee as soon as it's ready." Before Dory could agree or disagree, Lily was pushing the stroller ahead of her and around to the rear of the building. Duke had made three trips to the back and now, with the exception of her luggage, the station wagon was empty. Brawn certainly did have its merits. She couldn't help wondering how artful he was in bed. If Sylvia's Cheshire-cat smile was any indication, he performed admirably. Sylvia would never settle for less than the best. I wonder if Griff knows, Dory muttered to herself as she trudged behind Lily, lugging two heavy suitcases. Sylvia's trilling voice and Duke's phony Texas twang grated on her ears. Damn, she wanted to see Griff. She didn't need Lily and her baby or Sylvia and her Saks wardrobe and alleycat appetites.

Inside the town house Lily was unpacking muffins wrapped in waxed paper, Saran wrap and tinfoil. She spread colorful checkered paper napkins to match the paper plates on one of the packed cartons. Dory fought the urge to tell her to leave. The phone shrilled to life and so did little Ricky. Lily tried to quiet the squealing baby as Dory strained to hear Griff's words.

"Oh, darling, it's so good to hear from you. I just this minute got here and Sylvia said . . . Sylvia said . . . When are you coming home, Griff?" she all but cried.

"Not till tomorrow. I just wanted you to know I'm think-ing about you and I can't wait to see you. This will give you a chance to start your decorating without me underfoot."

"What did you say, Griff? I can't hear with the baby crying and all." She sent Lily a murderous look that went right over the young woman's head. The more she crooned, the louder little Ricky shrieked.

"He does have a good pair of lungs, doesn't he?" Griff laughed.

"What? Talk louder, I can't hear you."

"Never mind, darling. I'll see you tomorrow. Tomorrow, darling."

"God damn it to hell, Lily, that was Griff. Couldn't you keep that kid quiet for two minutes? I have no idea what he said to me," Dory wailed. She felt like throwing a tantrum to equal little Ricky's. Instead she sat down with her back against the wall and bit into one of the moist muffins. Lily waited expectantly for her comment. Evidently, Dory's sharp words about her baby had fallen on deaf ears.

"Good. Very good," Dory muttered. Lily frowned. "Delicious. Are they difficult to make?" she babbled. "Can you make them in a microwave oven?"

"Do you really think they're good? I spent all last evening making them for today. I brought enough for Griff too, so you won't have to worry about breakfast tomorrow."

Dory ignored her as Sylvia tripped into the kitchen on her three-inch heels. The skin-tight, lime-green coverall was made of silk and clung to Sylvia as though it had been painted on. Three strands of real pearls graced her throat. Dory would have parted with her eye teeth for just one of the strands. The pearls were worth at least four thousand dollars and the coverall around three hundred. She wondered how much John paid for his clothes.

"Here we are, kiddies, piping hot coffee. I'd like to stay and chat, but I have to go to the hairdresser and then I have an appointment for a pedicure. I'll give you a call tomorrow, Dory, to see how things are."

"You just went to the hairdresser day before yesterday," Lily grumbled.

"Darling, I refuse to look dowdy or matronly. It wouldn't hurt you to pay more attention to your own looks. You need a rinse and isn't it time you stopped nursing that child? You look positively . . . fat. You have to start thinking about your figure now."

"Why? Rick hasn't complained. I'll work on it when little Ricky is older. I want to enjoy every minute of him and nurse him as long as I can."

"You're a fool," Sylvia said curtly. "I love you, Lily, but you are a homemaking fool. Still, somebody has to do it." With a breezy wave of her hand Sylvia was gone, her heels clicking on the flagstone walkway.

"I just bet she slept with that . . . that . . . jockey," Lily said through pursed lips. "How could she?"

"It's easy, you take off your clothes and slip between the sheets. Isn't that how you got little Ricky?" Dory sniped. God, what was happening to her? Had she really said that to Lily? Evidently she had, for tears welled up in Lily's eyes. "Look, it isn't your business or mine. I'm sorry. Let's forget it. Why don't you take little Ricky home? I can manage and I'd like to be alone for a while. I'm also very tired."

"But Rick said I should stay and help you," Lily complained. "He'll be upset with me if I don't help you."

Dory lost what little patience she had left. "Then for God's sake don't tell him. The baby looks sleepy. You go along now and I'll manage very well. Thanks for thinking of me with the muffins. I would like the recipe, if you don't mind."

Lily's world was suddenly right side up. Her face lit like a beacon. "I'll call you as soon as I get home and give it to you. You're sure now that I can't do anything?"

"Not a thing. Go along now," Dory said in a motherly tone.

The moment Lily and the baby were out of sight, Dory locked the back door and sighed with relief. Now, damn it, she could cry. She could cry or bawl or stamp her feet and bawl at the same time. Instead, she rummaged in one of the cartons till she found a fat silken comforter. She carried it upstairs to the bedroom. She spread it out by the fireplace and lay down. She had time for a short nap before the movers arrived. Tears clung to her lashes as she closed her eyes in sleep.

Dory felt as though she had just closed her eyes when the phone jangled. Thinking it was Griff, she crawled groggily across the room. "Hello," she said sleepily.

"Dory, it's Lily. I just got home and I'm calling like I promised, to give you the muffin recipe. Do you have a pencil?"

"Of course," Dory lied. Why me, she said silently, her eyes raised upward. She listened patiently while Lily read off ingredients and measurements. "Thank you, Lily," she mumbled between clenched teeth.

Sleep was out of the question now. She might as well get up, change her clothes and get to work. Maybe Griff would change his mind and make it home tonight after all. If she could entice the movers to set up the bed and place the furniture, she could get on with the unpacking.

It was late afternoon when she realized she was hungry. Dory looked around to survey her handiwork. She felt pleased with herself. She had definitely made inroads. Tomorrow the drapery people would hang the curtains and the surprise chair she had purchased for Griff would arrive. Covered in a deep plum velour, it would give his study just the touch of color needed to make the room restful and yet attractive. He was going to be so surprised. She smiled to herself as she envisioned the way he would pick her up and twirl her around, his eyes laughing merrily. Then he would say, "How did you know this was exactly what I wanted?" And then she would say, "Because I think like you do and can read your mind." They would kiss, a long, searing, burning, mind-reeling kiss, and then they would go to bed and make the universe tilt the way it always did. If I don't get some food, Dory thought, I won't have the strength to kiss him, much less tilt universes.

She backed the station wagon out of the parking spot and headed back toward Jefferson Davis Parkway. She drove till she came to Fern Terrace and Ollie's Trolley. It was a real trolley car, converted into a diner, and Ollie had the best chili dogs on the eastern seaboard. At least that's what his sign proclaimed. Dory tested his advertisement and agreed. Two chili dogs, one giant root beer and one envelope of greasy French fries made her burp with pleasure. "Ollie," Dory said as she paid her check, "you are indeed a prince among men. You deliver what you promise. I think these were the best hot dogs I've ever eaten."

The man named Ollie threw back his head and laughed. He had baby-fine hair that barely covered his scalp and an infectious laugh, and Dory found herself joining in. "I get people from all over. Secret is in just serving what you advertise. When you add to your menu, that's when you get into trouble. As you noticed, the French fries leave a lot to be desired, but I have to serve them. Kids demand French fries. You were lucky, I was just getting ready to close up. Good day today. I had two senators and the secretary of the navy sent his aide for a batch of my dogs. The Pentagon is my best customer. You take that Senator Collins. He comes here three times a week. He says he's never getting married as long as I stay in business."

Dory's ears perked up. "He's the young good looking one from somewhere in New England, isn't he? A bachelor and the youngest man in the Senate, right?"

"That's the one," Ollie said, packing up his stained wrap-around apron in a plastic bag for his wife to wash.

"Three days a week, huh?"

"Yep. Why, a person could just stop by, say around one-ish and you'll find him leaning against the trolley eating three dogs. Always has two root beers. Never touches the French fries. Says the grease gives him zits. He's always gettin' his picture took and he don't want no . . . blemishes marking up that good lookin' face of his. You new around here?" he asked, shoving his money bag into his plastic carryall.

"Just moved in today. I live over in the town houses on Jeff Davis Parkway. My name's Dory Faraday," she said, holding out her hand.

"Nick Papopolous, a.k.a. Ollie," Nick said, offering her a hand and arm as large as a railroad tie. "Come on, I'll walk you to your car. Lots of loonies around here." To prove his point, he withdrew a heavy-looking black gun and shoved it into his belt. He didn't bother to pull his shirt down over the weapon, preferring to let it show. "I got a permit for this," he said, pulling the door closed behind him.

Dory watched in awe as he tossed his plastic bag full of money and his dirty apron into the back of a Mercedes 380SL. The hot dog business must be good, Dory thought as she guided the station wagon out of the parking lot. Drake Collins, the newest, the youngest, the sexiest senator on Capitol Hill. *Soiree* would love him. Unattached, brilliant, going far, eye on the governor's chair. What more could a girl want, especially an unemployed girl. Woman. Career person. *Soiree* reader. *Soiree* was aimed at the successful woman and was rated second only to *Time*. Collins was perfect for her first *Soiree* profile. She would definitely make it her business to lunch at Ollie's Trolley every chance she got. But first things first. She had to finish the house and start school.

For some reason she felt annoyed and out of sorts when she got back to the house. The boxes of books made her frown. She had to find a place for them until she could have some shelves installed. One more day to herself before she hit the classroom. Even though she was late, she would catch up. She would have to!

Dory made up the bed, showered and washed her hair. Wrapped in a cheerful lemon-colored robe, she gazed down at the bold geometrics of slate greys and umber browns on the crisp sheets and pillowcases. Griff loved this particular set of sheets, saying they made him want to do wild, impetuous things to her. She was propping the pillows up so she could read when the phone suddenly rang. It had to be Griff saying good-night. She smiled as she picked up the phone. Her voice was a low, sensuous purr. "I miss you, darling," she said, leaning back into her nest of pillows.

"You'd be in big trouble if it wasn't me on the phone," Griff laughed.

"Who else would be calling me after dark? I really don't want to complain but this bed is so big and I'm not taking up much room. I wish you were here."

"I do too, honey. But I've got my work carved out for me here. This was a golden opportunity that was too good to refuse. It just came at a bad time. I'm sorry. There's eleven thoroughbred horses in the senator's stables, and this afternoon I began inducing labor in one of his prize mares. By noon tomorrow she should drop a fine colt."

Dory bristled. Normally, she loved to hear Griff talk about his work. She loved animals too, but this . . . this was too much. She had just propositioned him over the phone, and he was telling her about a prize mare and eleven thoroughbreds. Even as she thought it, Dory felt ashamed. Just because her needs weren't being met was no reason to get her back up. Griff had needs too.

"Dory?" his voice questioned. "Are you there?"

"I'm here, Griff."

"You're not angry, are you? Tell me you understand, Dory."

"I do, Griff. It's just that this would have been our first night together in our own house. I thought you would carry me over the threshhold and we could have some wine. You'd light the fireplace in the bedroom and we'd make long, lazy love. But it's all right. I understand."

Griff's groan was clearly audible. Dory felt smug. At least now he knew what he was missing. "We'll do that tomorrow night and that's a promise. Now that you've churned me all up, I'm going to have to take a cold shower. By the way, did Sylvia give you a hand today? She offered to help."

Dory thought of Sylvia and then of Duke and the smitten looks on both their faces. "Yes, Sylvia helped," Dory said grudgingly. Helped herself is what she did, the nasty thought concluded.

"She's something. I think she's one of those people you can always count on in a pinch," Griff was saying. "Look how she hunted apartments for us."

"Hmmmm. I suppose." And look what the wonderful Sylvia came up with, Dory grimaced, thinking of that last especially unattractive apartment house complete with Sylvia's own brand of grime.

"Remember now, we have a date for tomorrow night. I'll give you a call sometime during the day if I get a chance. I love you, Dory."

It was on the tip of her tongue to give her usual response of "I love you, darling" but she didn't. Instead she said, "Me too."

Dory lay for a long time staring at the ominous jacket of John Saul's latest book. Tomorrow wouldn't be the same. Tomorrow was tomorrow and this was now. Today. The *first* night. How could tomorrow possibly be the same? She felt cheated. Angry and cheated. And she didn't like it.

She opened the book with a dramatic flourish. And just what did one do for a horse in labor that took the entire night? Priorities. Order of preference. She came after a horse. And induced labor? The thought just struck her. If Griff had had to induce the labor, couldn't it have waited until tomorrow? He was setting the timetable, not Mother Nature!

Her eyes snapped and chewed at the words written by Saul, not comprehending, not caring. Angrily, Dory leapt from the bed, the new book skidding to the floor. She ripped the geometric sheets from the bed and carried them to a white wicker hamper in the dressing room. She replaced them with a frilly set of lacy ruffled sheets and pulled them up haphazardly. These sheets were designed with a single woman in mind. Extravagantly feminine, too lush, too Victorian to make a man feel comfortable.

Sitting alone on her girlish bed didn't make her feel a hell of a lot better. Griff could have talked to her longer. He could have said more. Been more romantic. Groans didn't count. He could have asked her how her day went, how she had made the trip down from New York. How the house was coming. He could even have asked about his station wagon! For all he knew, she could have had an accident. Sylvia. Horses. He was only allowing himself a precious few minutes to talk to the woman he said he loved, and yet he talked about a horse she didn't even know and a woman she wasn't certain she even liked.

She wouldn't cry. What was the point? To feel better? Would tears really make the hurt go away? Too bad she didn't have a Band-Aid big enough to ease the pain she was feeling. Was she expecting too much? Would she be feeling the same way if they were married and this happened? Griff had priorities, but so did she, damn it. If she could put him first, why couldn't he put her first?

What really hurt was the fact that she was disappointed in Griff. Not in the circumstances, but in Griff himself. Was it unrealistic to expect the man you love to come home on the first night and make love to you? No, and tomorrow wouldn't be the same. How could Griff think it would be? For God's sake, she wasn't sitting here waiting to be seduced. Their relationship was beyond that stage.

She felt as if she had been put through a mill and had come out mangled and smashed. It was so damn easy to pick up the phone and make a call, sure in the knowledge that the other person would understand and forgive. Forgive yes; forget, no. When you hurt you don't forget, she told herself. And when you're taken for granted, you don't forget that either.

Despite her resolution not to cry the tears trickled down her cheeks. She wanted him to *want* to come home to her. She didn't care about priorities, she didn't want to think about them. All she wanted was Griff here beside her. She wanted him here telling her he loved her and it was right, this move to D.C. Goddamn it, she needed reassurance. Second fiddle to a horse. Wait till Pixie heard about this one.

Sleep would never come now. She should get up and watch television till she worked off her hostility. Or better yet, have a few snorts from the bottle of brandy Pixie had given her.

Now, if she could just remember where she had put it, she could get pleasantly sloshed. Snookered, maybe. On second thought, three aspirins would be better, she decided. Besides, she had promised herself to save the brandy to toast Pixie's story.

Dory punched the pillow with a vengeance. She was angry, frustrated, *out of control*. The thought made her rigid. Eventually, she slept, her dreams panicked by a wild-eyed stallion carrying Sylvia on his back as he raced up and down Jefferson Davis Parkway. She woke exhausted.

Chapter Four

THE DRAPERIES WERE HUNG AND PINNED BY NOON; THE NEW chair for Griff's den was delivered. Both Lily and Sylvia called to invite her to lunch. She begged off, saying she had to do some grocery shopping and pick up a map so she could find her way to Georgetown University the next day. "I want to make Griff's favorite dinner, so I don't have all that much time," she told Sylvia.

"Are you going to freeze it?" Sylvia asked indifferently.

"No, why?"

"I just spoke to John and he said they wouldn't be home till late this evening. We were invited out for drinks and dinner, and now I either have to go alone or cancel. I don't suppose you'd like to go with me, would you? Griff suggested I ask you."

Out of control, out of control, her mind screamed as Sylvia rattled on about how she had told Griff Dory wasn't ready yet for the social scene and to give her time.

Dory floundered. "Well then, I'll just have a snack and get my things ready for tomorrow. First day of school. Thanks for calling, Sylvia. I appreciate the invitation, but some other time." She broke the connection, not waiting for Sylvia's reply.

Lily's phone call was an invitation also. She wanted Dory to come over and watch her make quince jelly, Rick's favorite. "I thought we could have tea and I'd make some fresh crumpets or scones. Little Ricky is so good in the afternoon, he just plays in his crib. We could have a nice long talk and really get to know one another.''

Dory rattled off a list of real and imaginary things she had to do. When she hung up the phone she felt as though she had done ten laps in a whirlpool. Upstream!

She was on her way out the door when the phone rang a third time. Dory debated for four rings before she picked up the receiver. Her voice was controlled. It was Griff, a cheerful Griff, asking how she was and what she was doing.

''Not much. I was just going to the supermarket, if I can find it, that is. I understand you won't be home for dinner.''

''I hope you don't mind. I should be home around nine-thirty or so. Just fix me a sandwich. Remember now, we have a date.''

''I haven't forgotten,'' Dory said lightly. Damn, why did his voice sound so preoccupied? He was saying words but his mind was somewhere else. She could tell. ''What kind of sandwich would you like?''

''What? Oh, anything. Pastrami and corned beef on rye would be good. Don't overdo, darling. Save some of your energy for this evening. I have to run now—the others are waiting for me. Love you.''

Dory replaced the phone and stared at it for a long, mesmerizing minute. Day two and already there was trouble in paradise. No one had said it would be easy. Adjustments all the way. With her doing the adjusting. Lizzie had tried to warn her. Katy had been right on target when she said, ''A woman gives ninety percent to every relationship. The man gives five percent and the dog the other five.'' Dory wondered what happened to the last five percent if one didn't have a dog.

All the way to the supermarket she told herself she was just feeling sorry for herself because she was alone with nothing to do. Nothing mental, that is. Physical work always frustrated her. She wasn't using her mind.

Tonight when she saw Griff things would be different. If they weren't different, this arrangement wasn't going to work. She would give fifty percent, maybe sixty percent, but that was her bottom line. She was getting off the track here. It was time to restructure her thinking before something serious happened. So what if Griff had to work late and be away? It was his job and she had said she understood.

She was being selfish. Selfish and childish. It had been a long time since she had answered to anyone, if there ever had been a time. The only person she had to please or defend was herself. Now she was thrust into a new ball game where there was a second player and she was going to have to adjust and realize she couldn't have everything her own way. No snapping of the fingers and getting whatever she wanted. And what did she want? To be happy with Griff. To be with Griff. To share Griff's life. That was what she wanted. So what if she didn't like some of the adjustments? She could live with that. She could adjust. In her own way.

Dory felt better immediately. She would surprise Griff and make a late dinner. Something that could hold and not be ruined if he was late. She would put the little rosewood table that had been her grandmother's in front of the living room fireplace. The new placemats and napkins, of course, and she would wear her cashmere lounging robe and dab the new, exotic perfume she hadn't used yet behind each ear and into the deep V of her breasts. She would seduce him first with her dinner and then with her body. She giggled to herself as she walked up and down the aisles of the supermarket, tossing in items helter-skelter. She bought all the ingredients for a succulent lamb stew and the makings for bread. Now, all she had to do was go home and get out her cookbook. If all else failed, she could always call the obliging Lily.

Dory watched in awe as the totals came to life on the cash register. How could she have spent one hundred sixteen dollars on four bags of groceries? Cooking certainly was expensive. She whipped out her Gucci wallet from her Gucci handbag and paid the bill. She felt momentarily deflated. She could have bought a silk blouse at Bloomingdale's for one hundred sixteen dollars. She would talk to Griff about groceries when she got a chance. They would have to arrive at some manner of sharing the bills.

On the drive back to the house she let her mind race up and down an invisible column of figures. Drapes, the chair for Griff, the new sheets and towels she had bought at Saks before coming down here, the odds and ends from Macy's Cellar, the deposits for the utilities, the cost of tuition and registration, not to mention the books she would have to buy, and now this one hundred sixteen dollars. The invisible sum stunned her. A quarter of a new fall wardrobe; a down payment on a mink coat; twenty-eight pairs of shoes. This new life wasn't a mistake, was it? This was unusual for her, this vacillation. What was wrong with her? No one forced her to come here; it was her own decision. That was it, the word "decision." Was it the wrong one? She couldn't think about all that now. Now she had to think about cooking dinner: lamb stew with homemade bread. Peach pie for dessert. Coffee and then a drink in front of the fireplace. The congressional aide had left plenty of logs for her use. It was going to be perfect, and then tomorrow, bright and early, she would start her studies at Georgetown. Pursuing her studies had to take top priority. God, how she was beginning to hate that word. Nothing and no one was going to rain on *her* parade.

By five-thirty the lamb stew was simmering, the peach pie was baking, and Dory was patting two loaves of bread into baking pans. She was smeared from head to toe with flour. This cooking was a bit much, in her opinion. She didn't see how women did it every day, three times a day.

While the dishes and pots and pans soaked she would change her clothes and put on her lounging robe. The worst part of the work was over now. She looked in dismay at her smudged and wrinkled shirt and flour-smeared jeans. Even her tattered sneakers from college wore a light dusting of flour. Her hair was tied back with a piece of string, and she looked a mess.

Novice that she was in the kitchen, Dory checked everything and set all the timers twice before she felt safe enough to fill the tub for a long, leisurely bath. Lord, she was tired. She should sleep like a log tonight. For more reasons than one, she smiled to herself as she made her way upstairs. She was halfway up when she heard a key in the lock. Wide-eyed, unable to move, she stood frozen on the steps and waited to see who it was that dared invade her new home.

"Griff!" It couldn't be Griff. It was Griff. He couldn't see her looking like this. But he was seeing her like this—and what was that strange look in his eye? Disbelief. By God, it was disbelief.

"Dory?" It was a question and a statement all in one.

Wild thoughts careered around in Dory's head. "Hi, darling. I was just going up to take a bath. Now that you're here, why don't you join me in a nice hot shower?"

"What I need is a drink, not a shower. Something smells good."

"Lamb stew, peach pie and homemade bread. I think it's the bread that smells so good."

"I bet you even churned the butter," Griff said lazily as he smiled at Dory's flour smudged face.

"That's next week," she grinned, rubbing her nose with the back of her hand. "I didn't expect you till later." She realized suddenly how stiff the words had sounded. Almost like an accusation. Was she always going to hear about Griff's schedule and plans first from either Sylvia or Lily? Was it only an afterthought on Griff's part to call her and tell her himself? "I'm such a mess," Dory blurted, hoping the edge had left her voice. "Oh, Griff, I wanted everything to be so special for your first night at home. You've caught me at my worst."

"I thought we were having baloney sandwiches," he grinned, gathering her into his arms. Apparently, he hadn't noticed the recrimination in her tone.

"You said pastrami and corned beef. I thought this would be better." Dory snuggled closer into his embrace. "If you're going to work all kinds of crazy hours, you need good, substantial food. Also, you better enjoy it now because when I start school you *will* be eating baloney sandwiches. Kiss me like you haven't seen me for ten days."

"On second thought," Griff told her, rubbing his mustache on the tip of her nose, making her wrinkle it against the tickling, "maybe a nice warm shower would be a good idea." He picked her up in his arms and carried her up the stairs. "This is in lieu of carrying you over the threshhold last night."

Contented, Dory cuddled in his arms, already anticipating the warm sting of the shower spray and Griff's warmer hands on her body.

Wrapped in her cozy, lemon-yellow terry robe, Dory sipped her wine while she watched Griff wolf down his dinner. His appetite would have to serve her as proof of his approval, for the words were not forthcoming. Even little promptings like, "I hope the stew is seasoned to your taste," and "don't you think the bread is a bit overdone?" only brought incoherent grunts that neither agreed nor disagreed.

This certainly wasn't the romantic evening Dory had envisioned. Their gymnastic lovemaking in the shower was rushed and somehow unsatisfying. The wine and candlelight, which should have been conducive to quiet conversation and romance, served instead as background for the TV news program Griff wanted to watch. Dory glanced longingly at the stereo and the carefully chosen stack of mood-music records she had planned to play.

Competing with the television for Griff's attention, Dory tried conversation. "You never told me what kept you at that senator's farm," she said softly, compelling him with her green eyes to turn his attention away from the television. The plight of welfare mothers did not seem to fit in with the sumptuous meal she had prepared.

"Hmmm? Oh, well, our little colt was extremely shy about making his debut into this world. I think I told you the mare should have delivered before noon today. She didn't make her presentation until almost three in the afternoon. Then we had to fight the traffic back into the city. Fine little colt. The senator raises quarter horses, as well as thoroughbreds, and he has lots of friends with the same interests. His recommendations should be a boon to the clinic."

"How did your clinic get involved, Griff? Wasn't the senator happy with the veterinarians he'd been using?"

"Actually, it was Sylvia and some of her connections that pulled it through for us. I don't have to tell you, honey, breaking into any business in the D.C. area can be tough. There's so much competition. We have Sylvia to be grateful to for this little venture. Fortunately, everything worked out well for the mare and her foal. John and I were quite concerned that inducing labor at the wrong stage of pregnancy could invite a breech birth. Tough on the mother and the baby."

An unreasoning chord of jealousy struck Dory. Griff was so damn grateful to Sylvia. She was almost tempted to shatter his regard for the woman by revealing what she suspected between Sylvia and Duke. What's happening to me? Dory thought, aghast. I've never been greedy for petty gossip! I never make judgments and betray other people, especially with the intention of destroying their reputations. Dory was terribly disappointed in herself and was only glad she'd stopped herself in time to keep her suspicions to herself.

"Did Rick join you and John out at the farm?" Her inquiry was made in a shaking voice. Dory was having doubts about herself and her motives. The whole center of her values seemed to have suddenly shifted. Why? Before she could answer herself, Griff was speaking.

"No, Rick didn't come out to the farm. You see the way he is with little Rick and Lily. John and I thought it would be an unnecessary imposition on their family."

"Lily is certainly wrapped up in her 'two men' as she calls Rick and the baby. Do you think it's good? I mean, certainly a woman should have something else in her life besides mothering and blueberry muffins."

Griff dug heartily into another slice of bread, lathering it thickly with butter. He seemed distracted both by the bread and the news commentary, and he didn't answer Dory's question until he'd taken another sip of wine. "I'm not so sure, Dory. Lily is of that special breed who seems most a woman when she's making a home for her man. Rick certainly adores her, as you can tell."

"I'm not asking what's good for Rick, darling. I'm asking what's good for Lily."

Griff smiled, his eyes lighting, a silly smile spreading beneath his sexy mustache. "I *am* talking about what's good for Lily. That girl positively blooms. And didn't I already tell you how John and I relieved Rick of responsibility out at the farm so he could be home with Lily and the baby? If that's not good for Lily, I don't know what is."

Dory returned his smile somewhat sheepishly. She didn't want to spoil this night with a contest of opinions, but she couldn't help thinking that Rick and Lily had already had so much time together. They were already a family. But last night had been Dory's first night in her new home, and that didn't seem to cut any ice with either John or Griff. What was it about Lily that made the partners want to protect her and make her happy? Was it simply that she was the typical "little woman"? What was it about herself that seemed to make it unnecessary for Griff to take special consideration of her, that left him guiltless about spending what should have been a special night for them by nursing a pregnant horse? Did she give the appearance of being totally self-sufficient and understanding about career and responsibility coming first? Dory stood abruptly and began clearing the table. She didn't like herself very much this evening and she wasn't quite certain what to do about it. Why should Sylvia be praised for being cosmopolitan and social climbing and Lily be idolized for being the perfect wife and mother? What about her, Dory? And when, if ever, was Griff going to comment on her efforts to make a home for them?

The dishes clattered into the sink. Taking a deep breath, Dory tried to rationalize. She was an intelligent woman, but right now she needed some focus to her life that was separate from her activities of setting up a home. Focus. That was what she was used to. Focus on her job, on the people she worked with, on Griff. She simply had to get these things back into perspective. Tomorrow, she promised herself. School, new people, new things to learn and study. Tomorrow, it would be all right.

79

Chapter Five

GRIFF LEFT FOR THE CLINIC EARLY IN THE MORNING, KISSING
Dory good-by as she put their coffee cups into the dishwasher.
"Here's for luck your first day of school. Nervous?"

"You bet. It's been some while since I've sat in a classroom,
don't forget. But I think there's still some life in the old gray
matter," she laughed, tapping her head.

Dory was nervous, more than she cared to admit. After
Griff left the house she found herself compulsively straighten-
ing cushions and smoothing the bed and giving another swipe
of the dishcloth to an already clean white formica counter.
She walked through the house, trying to see the results of her
efforts through objective eyes. The soft gray carpeting in the
living room picked up the gentle pinks and buffered whites in
the Italian marble fireplace. Most of the furnishings from her
apartment in New York were already in place; only a few
decorator items and knickknacks were still left to be unpacked.
The chrome and glass étagère and end tables from Griff's loft
added a striking note of contrast against her more formal
traditional pieces of white velvet and damask. She could run
into town today and see if she could pick up some toss
pillows, a few in the same shade as the carpeting and others
in that deep plum color she liked so well. Perhaps she could
order several huge stack cushions in plum velvet to serve as
extra seating. Her collection of crystal paperweights would
look terrific on the glass table banked against the sofa.

Dory shook her head. What was she doing standing here decorating the living room when she should be upstairs this minute getting dressed?

Up the carpeted stairs and down the short hallway, Dory entered the bedroom which, along with its accompanying dressing room and bath, comprised the entire second floor of the town house. There was still much work to be done here. New drapes to be hung, deciding on the accent colors, finding a love seat and easy chair to place before the fireplace. She must see about finding a wax or a finishing compound to bring out the best in the ornately designed andirons. Set with white fieldstone, the fireplace was built into a stuccoed wall and centered on the far side of the room. A really striking tapestry or rug would be just the thing to hang over the hearth.

Dory's eye caught the movement of the digital alarm clock on the bedside table. If she didn't hurry, she would be late for school. The city map she had bought made finding the university easy, but she still didn't know about parking or even how to find the buildings where her classes were to be held.

Rifling through her drawers to find underwear and stockings, Dory chewed her bottom lip with worry. She had had every intention of driving out to Georgetown yesterday to get the lay of the land, but somehow she hadn't done it. Why had she allowed herself to become distracted by household chores and preparing that extravagant dinner? Griff had told her he would be more than satisfied with sandwiches. She could have put her time to better use.

Rushing for the bathroom and turning on the shower, Dory berated herself for not making her priorities stand. She never should have let herself be sidetracked. She detested being late, and even judged others by how promptly they kept appointments. Stepping under the steaming spray, she pushed back the thought that perhaps her dallying around the house with her various chores might be an indication that she was not as eager to go back to school as she had thought.

Midway through the first day of school Dory had what Griff later described as an anxiety attack. It hit her when she

81

was walking from one building to the next shortly after the lunch hour. She felt weak and her head reeled. The first thought that ricocheted through her brain was that she was pregnant. Then she realized how ridiculous the thought was and felt worse. She sat down on a bench until the dizziness passed, her heart fluttering wildly. By the time she teetered to her class she had herself diagnosed and was making out a will in her mind. She was to be cremated and . . . God, what would they do with her ashes? Her parents might want them or Aunt Pixie might find some use for them. Griff wanting her ashes never occurred to her. If she was going to die, why was she sitting here in this damn dumb, stupid class trying to convince herself and the instructor that she did indeed want to get her doctorate? As the courtroom voice of the professor droned on, Dory let her mind wander. Some inner sense told her that there was nothing wrong with her, physically. It was nerves, it was all too much, too quick, too fast. She hadn't adjusted yet. Time. She needed time.

Time was measured by clocks and calendars, things she had worked with for years. She had always watched the clock, ticked off the days on the calendar, made a schedule and stuck to it. Now, she felt adrift.

When the class was over Dory hadn't the faintest idea of what had been said or who sat next to her. The instructor was almost out the door before she got up from her seat. Thank God she had taped the class. She switched the button on the small Sony recorder and slipped it into her bag. She felt rotten. Not physically rotten. Just rotten. She glanced at her watch and wondered what Katy and the others were doing. If she really wanted to know, she could call up and find out. She didn't really want to know, she told herself as she walked down the hall looking for a student lounge. A cup of coffee would help. Maybe some crackers or something to settle her churning stomach. She was behaving worse than a child on the first day of school.

Dory suffered through a two-hour lecture on Chaucer's boyhood, watching the minute hand on her watch. The instructor walked up and down in front of the class, tapping a pencil against his fat pink palm. It might have helped her concentration if he was handsome with good teeth. It was no fun to look at a middle-aged, balding man with baggy trousers. There was even a shine to his pants. For shame on his wife, Dory thought. His white shirt was polyester, and gray with repeated washings. Ring around the collar, no doubt. Lily would know how to make the shirt clean again. Little Ricky's bibs were so blindingly white they hurt the eyes. She wondered what Lily was doing. Where was Sylvia? She wished she was with Griff.

Her palms were starting to sweat again. By forcing herself to stare at the instructor's shirt front she was able to control the attack of dizziness. Think about something pleasant, anything. A meadow of daisies. A clear sparkling lake filled with jumping fish. Christmas with Pixie and a mound of presents. Damn it to hell, why wasn't it working? Why was her throat closing? My God, what if she collapsed? She tried clearing her throat and got an annoyed glance from the instructor. Her throat constricted again and she could feel the saliva building up in her mouth. Oh God, don't let me drool, not here in front of all these people. Was it her imagination or were people staring at her as she dabbed at her wet mouth?

To get up now and walk out would only call attention to herself. Better to sit still and try to concentrate on the lecture. Why was this instructor so damn long-winded? Didn't they cut classes short anymore? She wanted to cry when she felt her throat muscles relax. She drew in deep breaths and exhaled slowly. She felt a little better. Thank God.

Dory looked around at the other students. They all wore rapt expressions. None of them was having an anxiety attack or whatever it was she was having. None of their minds appeared to be wandering the way hers was. They seemed to be accepting the instructor regardless of his looks and clothing. What was wrong with her? How could she be thinking about such ridiculous things? Or was this one more indication that she wasn't taking her doctorate seriously? Intentions, good or bad, were one thing; following through was something else entirely. She had to give that theory a lot of thought.

Dory was the first one out of the room when the professor nodded his head in the general direction of the class. Dismissed. Thank God. If she checked the map, she might have time to stop by the garden nursery she had noticed on her way to school. Autumn blooms and some plants for the house. There would be time to arrange them and place them to the best advantage. Also time for making a pot roast. Griff loved pot roast and so did she. Aunt Pixie always said if you added apple juice to the gravy, you had pure ambrosia.

She drove with the windows down. She felt wonderful with the crisp fall air whipping at her through the open window. She couldn't wait to get home and out of the tight, clinging silk slacks and Oscar de la Renta overblouse with matching belt. She kicked the two-hundred-dollar shoes off and wiggled her toes. She had to remember to buy some foot powder for her sneakers. And she needed more than one pair of sneaker socks. Back in New York she had only used the washers and dryers in the basement of the building once every three weeks or so. Everything else went to the cleaners. Now there were Griff's clothes to launder.

While the nursery man loaded the ferns, the philodendrons, and Swedish ivy into the back of the station wagon, Dory stared at the colorful blooms of the autumn flowers. To the right there was a decorative display of pumpkins and coppery colored chrysanthemums. On impulse, she bought the biggest pumpkin and four pots of the bronze flowers. Then she added one of the deep yellow and another of rich lavender. There was barely room in the car for herself. The owner was delighted with the check she wrote out for two hundred thirty dollars. She didn't bat an eye. It was worth it. Griff would love the flowers and the pumpkin. Everyone needed a fern at the kitchen window. Fireplaces always needed greenery on the hearth. Oh, what she could do with that fireplace come Christmas.

Back at the town house her silken garments slithered to the floor. The alligator shoes lay lopsidedly beside them. A lacy froth of powder blue bra found a home on the neat spread. Jewelry went back into the nest of velvet.

Dory stepped into faded jeans and a pullover shirt of deep orange. She liked the feeling against her skin. What a pleasure to go without underwear. A wicked grin split her features. If Griff liked all that froth and lace, he would love bare skin even more. She liked it when he ran his hand up under a blouse or shirt. God, he had such delicious hands.

The Halston case with its notebooks and cassette recorder landed with a thump on a coffee-colored slipper chair. Dory grimaced as she read her initials in gold lettering. Ostentatious, she thought.

Time to put the pot roast on. While it was browning, she would bring in the plants and arrange them. But when she was finished she felt disappointed. She should have bought more. A tree, a big leafy tree was called for, and she needed more fill-in plants. Damn, she had been so sure she had enough. If there was one thing she disliked, it was something that looked unfinished. A glance at the digital clock told her she had time to make a quick run back to the nursery. But first she called the clinic to see what time Griff would be home. He sounded annoyed when he said some time around seven. Dory barely noticed the annoyance as she calculated her driving time.

It was six o'clock when Dory backed the station wagon into her parking space. She struggled with the bushy tree and had to drag it into the house. The second tree, reed-slim with lacy pointed leaves, found its way to the living room. A second pumpkin and the three boxes of assorted fill-in plants sat next to the fireplace. When she was finished arranging them, she stifled the urge to call Lily to come for a look-see. Lily would love it. Sylvia would say, "Darling, it looks like a goddamn jungle and what do you mean, you wax the leaves?" Griff would be delighted and compliment her on making the town house look like a home. She decided not to mention that this batch of greenery had set her back another two hundred forty dollars. Trees were expensive but every leaf was worth the money. She would economize somewhere else.

Satisfied with her handiwork, Dory retreated to the kitchen

to wash the greens for a salad. Fresh string beans and four ears of corn would complete their meal. Dessert would be fresh pears soaked in brandy. Griff was going to love it, just love it.

Griff's mind was on the Interstate as he watched for the Arlington turnoff. John had to speak to him twice before he turned to look at the older man. "I'm sorry, John, what did you say?"

"I said Sylvia is going back to work at the beginning of the week. You know she likes to have her summers off for golf and tennis. It's not that she makes a fistful of money; actually, she uses up half of what she makes driving that gas guzzler of hers, but it makes her happy. I'm glad she's doing something for herself. It's important that women do things just for themselves. Makes them . . ." he sought for the word Sylvia had drilled into his head a hundred times. ". . . fulfilled. Of course, you know what I'm talking about. Dory is a career girl. And now that she's going back for her doctorate, you must be very proud of her, Griff. She'll definitely be an asset to you. Of course, Sylvia isn't anywhere near Dory's league, but selling cosmetics is something she likes, and Neiman-Marcus is a prestigious store."

Griff wondered why John sounded so defensive when he spoke of Sylvia and fulfillment. Dory as an asset. His eyebrows went up a fraction of an inch. "Dory is her own person, John. Always has been. I love her. I respect her intelligence. I admire her independence and the way she's climbed her way to the top of her field. I don't mind telling you I'm a little in awe of her now that she's going back to pursue her studies. She's probably the only person I know who is a 'whole' person. Capably whole."

John swiveled in his seat to stare at Griff. Was there a hint of something other than admiration in the man's voice? Surely, he couldn't be jealous of his . . . live-in. John always felt uncomfortable when he had to refer to Dory in a manner other than calling her by name. These live-in situations were not to his liking. In the end they always caused problems. Sylvia, with all her free-spirited ways, was probably even more suited to marriage than Lily. Sylvia liked being married. She preferred being Mrs. instead of Miss or Ms.

"I hope the girls hit it off and can do things together. Sylvia still has a lot of time on her hands. Lily has never managed to domesticate her, so it's up to Dory to take her in hand. Sylvia doesn't like to be pushy, if you know what I mean. She's going to stand back and give Dory room. You mark my word, those two are going to be good friends. You do think they'll hit it off, don't you?"

Griff noted the anxious tone of the older man. "I'm sure of it, John. But I do think we should let them pace it out themselves."

"Absolutely." John leaned back and closed his eyes. There was no sense in telling Griff that he was worried about Sylvia and the way she was spending her time *and* money. His money. It was nothing for her to drop two thousand dollars at the Galleria in one day. Even with wise and careful investing, he was going to have to draw the line with her. And, she was now annoyed when he asked her where she was and how she spent the day. He hated to use the word secretive, but it was the only word that applied to Sylvia these days. He also wasn't going to tell either Griff or Rick that he had joined a men's health club. His blood pressure was up and he had willingly given up salt and spicy foods. It wasn't too late, he assured himself. There was still time to put that lift in his step and beef himself up a bit. He had never been athletic and his lean body seemed to be shrinking into a kind of old man's stringiness. Sort of like a tough, old rooster.

"I think I'll tell Dory to put whatever she cooked for dinner in the fridge and take her out to dinner. I could use some ambiance this evening. Dory started school today and I know she's not going to be in the mood for much of anything. A nice, quiet dinner, just the two of us."

"Sounds good to me," John drawled. He wondered if Sylvia was going to serve Swanson's pot pies or make soup and sandwiches. Some day he was going to figure out how many cans of Campbell's soup he had consumed since marrying Sylvia. Christ, how he hated what Sylvia called grilled cheese sandwiches. White bread with a slice of cheese on a paper plate warmed in the microwave oven. Low-calorie yogurt on a stick was dessert seven days a week. But he loved her, heart and soul. It never occurred to him to complain. Sylvia wouldn't like it if he complained. When he complained Sylvia turned away from him in bed and spent money faster than he could breathe. He wondered who was going to take care of him in his twilight years. He smiled. Sylvia would hire the best nurse possible to wheel him around. She would check on him three times a day. The thought made him want to gag. I'm counting on Dory Faraday to bring some stability to my marriage, he admitted to himself. If it didn't work out, naturally he would bring pressure to bear on Griff. He wouldn't like doing it, but if it meant saving Sylvia from whatever she needed to be saved from, he would do it. In his gut he knew she wasn't sleeping around. Sylvia would never do that to him. She respected her marriage vows. He was *almost* sure of it. But why was she so restless, so lacking in serenity? He hoped Dory could find out.

Griff dropped John off and headed north toward his own home. The goddamn plum pits were still in the van. Sylvia's stale perfume curled his nostril hair. He fought off a fit of sneezing and turned on the air conditioning. It didn't help. Sylvia might be a class act, but she sure needed a lesson or two in the use of perfume. He wondered how John stood it.

The van slid in next to the station wagon. Walking around the back, he noticed the spilled dirt and broken leaves and branches in the back of the wagon. He frowned. He'd always been meticulous about his car. What in the hell had Dory been lugging around?

"Hi, honey, I'm home. What say we splurge and go out to dinner this evening?" Griff called out to Dory as he walked down the hall to the kitchen.

Dory stared at the thickening gravy of the pot roast and then at Griff. Griff's eyes took in the set table, the bubbling pots and Dory's flushed face. "You did all this and went to school too?" he asked in amazement.

Dory nodded happily. "Pot roast, gravy, string beans, corn on the cob and pears soaked in brandy for dessert. Do you still want to go out to dinner?" she teased.

"Hell no, only a fool would do a thing like that. How about a beer while I get ready to shower?"

"Go along and I'll bring it up to you. How did you like the living room?"

"Why, what did you do? I just headed straight down the hallway."

Dory uncapped a bottle of beer and trailed behind Griff. She couldn't wait to see his reaction.

"Honey, this is fantastic. How in the hell did you do all of this? I didn't know you were Superwoman."

"By working my tail off. I'm so glad you're pleased. Plants make all the difference. Tell me you like it, Griff."

"You did a great job, honey. Was it expensive?"

"Not really. I got some bargains and . . . the total was . . . around one hundred dollars or so," Dory lied.

"Fantastic. A bargain hunter too. I definitely approve. I knew I liked you for a reason. What time is dinner?"

"Dinner is whenever you finish your second beer," Dory said, kissing him lightly on the cheek.

Griff ate voraciously. He praised everything at least three times. Dory preened as he complimented her. She rattled on about the care and feeding of the plants and the amount of sunshine they needed, and how a grow light was a must. From there, she babbled on about the apple juice in the pot roast gravy and how she had, just by a stroke of luck, found the last corn of the season. Griff listened to every word, mesmerized by her excitement. "How did school go?" he asked when she slowed down to sip at her wine.

Dory frowned and told him about her dizzy spell. Griff stared at her with concern. "And you did all this when you got home? No more spells?"

"No. Never felt better. Nerves, I guess."

"Anxiety attack. Don't overdo, Dory. We have a year's lease. Take your time and don't push yourself. Promise me that if it happens again, you'll tell me and we'll get it checked out. I'm as sure as you are that it's just nerves, but it doesn't pay to leave anything to chance."

"It's sweet of you to be concerned, but I'm okay and I promise. Now tell me what you're going to do this evening? Do we watch television like an old married couple or do you have work to do in your den?"

"Honey, I have to go back to the clinic. We have a Kerry blue that had nine pups today, and they aren't doing all that well. Upper respiratory problems. They're such valuable dogs, I want to make sure we do everything possible for them. I'd do the same for a mutt, but these particular dogs belong to Senator Gregory. Politics, my dear." He grinned.

Dory's face fell. Her wonderful mood was shattered. Griff didn't seem to notice as he talked on about the Kerry blues. "I guess you'll have the den to yourself for studying. I shouldn't be too late. Around ten or ten thirty. I'll be back before you know it. By the time you get the kitchen cleaned up and do some studying, I'll be home, and then look out," he leered. "Say, why don't you call Sylvia? John told me she's about to go back to work at Neiman-Marcus. I know she'd love to hear from you."

"Okay, I'll do that," Dory promised as she started to clear the table. Griff pecked her on the cheek and left by the kitchen door. It was at times like this that Dory wished she smoked.

While the dishwasher sloshed its way through two rinse cycles Dory called Sylvia and chatted for a few minutes. "Darling, how nice of you to call. How was school?" Not waiting for a reply, Sylvia rattled on. "I always hated school. So Griff told you about my job. I just adore it. And," she said, laughing, "I get thirty percent off anything I buy. Let me know what you need. And, darling, when you have some free time and want to go shopping, just call me. I can show you the stores to stay away from. If Lily would just stop breast feeding that tot and get a sitter, we could have some wonderful times. I don't know about you, but I'm mortified every time she unhooks her bra. That baby just . . . guzzles and Lily always has this stupid look on her face as though she's orgasmic. Dis-gusting. I'd love to chat longer, but John and I are playing bridge with some friends this evening. Call me now," Sylvia said airily. Dory stared at the phone for a minute and then hung up. So much for Sylvia. Thirty percent off. That was good. She wondered if it applied to anything in the store or just cosmetics.

Dory stared at the phone, willing Sylvia's animated face to appear. What made Sylvia run? What was Sylvia all about? A little dose of Sylvia went a long way. She thought she knew what the older woman's problem was, if it was a problem. She feared old age, suffered from a fear of being unloved and ending up alone someday. Fear was the crack in Sylvia's veneer. Dory could understand that fear. It was something every woman could understand. It was the way a woman handled that fear that made the difference. Tolerant . . . that's what she must be, with Sylvia.

Dory sighed. She might as well call Lily too. She felt as though she needed an excuse. Her eyes fell to the trash can and the blueberry muffins she had thrown out. "Lily, I just wanted you to know Griff loved the muffins."

"Oh, I knew he would. Men always love anything homemade. How are you, Dory? I've been thinking about you all day and how I admire you going back to school and all. I wish I had the stamina to do it, but I'm locked in here with little Ricky and big Rick. Did Griff tell you about the Kerry blues? Rick said they're all worried about them. Wouldn't it be awful if all nine of them died?"

"Yes, it would. Sylvia told me she's going back to work. Isn't that wonderful?" God, it was hard to talk to Lily.

"I'm not sure if it's wonderful or not. Sylvia just pretends to work. She spends most of her time making up her face for the customers. I hardly find that work. In fact, I think it's dull. I rarely use cosmetics myself, Rick doesn't like them. So, when I do use them I use the organic kind."

"Somehow I knew you would." Dory's tart tone was lost on Lily.

"Dory, I'm starting to make quilt squares. I'm going to make a quilt for little Ricky. Quilting makes me feel so . . .

91

so Old American, you know, like in Colonial times or something. If you want to do one, we could work on them together. I have the pattern and loads of material. I save everything, all kinds of scraps. I have so much we could each make three quilts and I'd have some leftovers.''

"Lily, I'm all caught up in school and everything. It sounds . . . interesting. If I find the time, I'll be glad to give it a try. I better get going now, I have a lot of work to catch up on. I'll call you as soon as I have some free time.''

"Any time. I'm always here. Now, don't you work too hard. Those old teachers are slave drivers. I remember what it was like.''

Quilts. Quince jelly. Blueberry muffins. I bet she paints murals on little Ricky's wall too, Dory thought uncharitably as she turned off the kitchen light and headed for the den.

The tape cassette she had recorded in class was playing, but she listened with only half an ear. Curled up on the new recliner she had bought for Griff's den, Dory recalled her conversation with Lily and tried to figure out what it was about the young woman that irritated her. She had known other women, her mother included, who concentrated all efforts, physical and emotional, to the making of a home. Lily's devotion to home and husband wasn't really that unusual, so what was it?

The remainder of the recorded lecture went unheard as Dory pondered her own questions. Finally, after much soul searching, she decided that Lily's capabilities and unswerving sense of direction made Dory feel inferior and inept. Rick seemed so content and happy due to Lily's ministrations, and Dory wanted to put that same gleam in Griff's eyes.

This was silly, Dory chided herself. Of course Griff was happy. What was there to be unhappy about? The niggling thought that she had refused Griff's proposal of marriage crept into the back of her mind. Was it possible that Griff really needed the stability and contentment of a legal, committed relationship? Was this arrangement of theirs somehow threatening? Why wasn't she able to commit herself to marriage? If she was happy with Griff, why shouldn't she turn in her resignation to *Soiree* and plant her roots here in D.C.? Did Griff suspect her of always needing a back-door escape out of a situation, and was he right?

The sudden, unwelcome thought of David Harlow sent a shameful shudder down her spine. It was true, she was trying to cover all the angles, even to the point of compromising herself to Harlow by not making it perfectly clear that she could never have more than a professional interest in him and that she resented his implying that she might. Compromised. She had walked into his trap with her eyes open, and now Harlow was sitting back in New York thinking that when she returned as managing editor there would be after-hours recreation. Fool! Fool!

The sound of a key in the door made Dory jump in alarm. Griff! How long had she sat here? Her eyes flew to her watch. It was after nine and she still hadn't listened to the recorded lecture.

"Hi, I'm home!" Griff called.

Dory was on her feet and running out to the living room, throwing herself into Griff's arms.

"Hey, what's this?" he asked, holding her tightly, feeling the tremblings race down her spine. "What's the trouble, honey? Did something frighten you?"

Dory clung to Griff as if for dear life. That was the word—frightened. Scared to death. She wanted him to hold her and tell her it was all going to be all right, but she knew she couldn't express *what* frightened her. It was impossible to put it into words, or even to face the fears head on. Right this minute, she only knew she needed Griff's strength, his love, his support. She wanted to hide herself away in him, have him protect her from the world and from her self-doubts. Safe. She wanted to be safe!

Dory buried her face in the crook of Griff's neck, wrapping her arms around him, wanting to dissolve inside him. She began kissing him, frantic little kisses at first, then longer, more seductive caresses of her lips and tongue contrived to evoke his passions and responses.

Griff was overwhelmed by this display of emotion, but his

93

confusion was allayed and finally stilled by a more primal need which she stirred. Lifting her into his arms, he carried her up the staircase, taking her to their bed. Dory's insistent fingers worked the buttons on his shirt and the fastenings of his belt. She wanted him, she kept murmuring, breathlessly, almost desperately. Baring his chest to her hands, she caressed the smooth expanse of his skin, following her touch with moist, hungry explorations of her lips. Impatient with the confining fabric of their clothing, Dory practically ripped the garments from her body, turning back again to hurry Griff with his.

Feeling him against her, skin against skin, breath against breath, Dory stretched out beneath him, pressing herself into the strength of his embrace.

"Take me now, Griff!" she implored, thrashing wildly under his weight. "Please take me now!"

The desperate edge of her voice was disguised by the passion in her words. Griff covered her, rocking against her, feeling himself trapped in the grip of her thighs and the clutch of her arms. Her words echoed through his head; his love for her compelling him to satisfy her desires.

Dory tried to lose herself in the arms of the man she loved. She tried to hide in him, to make herself safe from those faceless shadows and self-doubts that pursued her.

Griff lay on his back, Dory's head resting peacefully on his shoulder. Something told him that only her body was at peace; something was very wrong for Dory. "Want to tell me about it?" he asked softly, caressing her arm with the flat of his hand, much the way one would soothe a child. He waited for her response; it was so long in coming, he thought she might not have heard him.

"No," Dory whispered at last. "This is something I've got to work out myself." Her cheeks bloomed pink in the darkness. Griff knew her well enough to know that something was very wrong. She had initiated their lovemaking with wild and wanton behavior and then ended in surrendering herself to him. Whatever she had done, it was different than it had ever been before. They had always been equals as lovers, giving and taking, pleasing and being pleased, finding in one another that special sensitivity which nurtures love and shares in the responsibility for it. Tonight, Dory was ashamed of herself. Tonight, she had used Griff to hide from her insecurities. Her body was sated, but there was a lingering feeling of failure. Tonight was different. Not better. Dory knew it and Griff knew it too.

Chapter Six

SEPTEMBER'S EXQUISITE INDIAN SUMMER DAYS GAVE WAY TO A sharper October complete with a kaleidoscope of autumn colors. Dory went to classes on a hit-and-miss basis, preferring to settle snugly into the town house poring over decorator books and gourmet recipes. She studied when the mood struck, often leaving it until early Monday morning while she did laundry. Sometimes, late at night after Griff was asleep, she would creep downstairs to pore guiltily through her notes and read assigned chapters.

In the morning, Griff would find her asleep at the desk. He'd kiss her consolingly and bring her coffee, saying, "Poor baby, you're really carrying quite a load, aren't you?"

Dory would protest heartily, pretending to slough off his commiserations. Although she crept down to the den with full intentions of studying, her real reason for getting up was that she couldn't sleep, knowing how she was neglecting her school work. But once settled in the den with soft music coming from the stereo, she would soon fall asleep. Nothing she read could penetrate the hateful malaise.

Griff was truly concerned. Dory had always been eager to share her life with him, telling him what was going on at the magazine and discussing new projects with him. Since coming to D.C. he'd noticed that she often became quiet, preferring to listen while he told about his day at the clinic and how business was increasing. It was tender and sweet, he decided, the way she listened so intensely to his recital of the day's events, and he had to admit he was selfish with her attention. But when he did ask her about her studies or her freelance projects for *Soiree* she would become quiet and introspective. He was quickly learning to shrug off Dory's lassitude. When he came right out and asked her if something was troubling her, she would look at him with that wide-eyed green stare of hers and offer denials. He might have pressed her further, following his instincts, if he weren't so involved and preoccupied with the clinic and his doubling patient file. That Dory was happy living with him, Griff had no doubt. She took pride in their home, was steeped in new ideas and color schemes, and she always sang or hummed tuneless little songs while she worked in the kitchen. Dory made their lives comfortable and cozy. It was just that she seemed to have taken on a burden—housekeeping, cooking, her studies, and her freelance work. When he thought of the subtle changes in her, a little frown would form between his brows.

Dory knew that Griff was concerned about her graduate work and her promised projects for *Soiree*. He always asked questions which she took great pains to dodge. How could she tell him that she was already weeks behind in her reading and that she hadn't even made the first contact for her magazine articles? It was easier to avoid the subject entirely. Just yesterday, she'd received a phone call from Katy, telling her *Soiree* had contacted several promising subjects for her, giving her the names and data on each. But when Katy began asking how things were going in D.C., Dory found an urgent excuse to cut the conversation short. She had heard the puzzlement in her friend's voice and several times during the day she had been tempted to call Katy back, but somehow she lacked the courage to pick up the phone. It occurred to Dory that she was actually hiding out, pulling the ground over her head. How could she converse about what she was doing and how she was doing it, when in truth she was doing nothing? She was disappointed in herself, angry actually, and was constantly vowing to get a grip on herself. Each night when she crawled into bed beside Griff she would experience deep shame and self-loathing because today had been no different from yesterday. It was only when she was buried in Griff's embrace, feeling his hands on her body and hearing the little love words he murmured, that she felt good about herself. She could hide away, even from herself, while she surrendered her body and her soul to the man she loved.

Shopping trips with Sylvia left her teeth on edge. It wasn't that she didn't enjoy the trips; she did. But the older woman's preoccupation with spending money in the shortest time possible annoyed her. If she was hiding, then Sylvia was hiding, too. She hid behind designer labels, costly makeup and secret trysts in the late mornings. Dory knew that shortly, inevitably, Sylvia was going to confide in her, and she didn't want to hear those confidences or be a part of them. Little by little she inched away from Sylvia and leaned more toward Lily. Lily was safe. With Lily she didn't have to think. Sylvia's blatant independence and bravado made Lily roll her eyes in dismay. "She's the most dependent person I know," Lily had smiled at Dory over a casserole lunch on the day before Halloween. "If you took John away, she would cave in and wither up like an apple."

Dory decided she almost liked Lily. Tolerating the plump young woman wasn't as difficult as it had been in the beginning. Take today, for example. She hadn't winced when Lily invited her for lunch to make scarecrows for the doorway. Halloween was such fun, she had said. Dory agreed, although she couldn't remember ever having much fun on the children's holiday. "It's little Ricky's first Halloween and I made him a Peter Cottontail costume," Lily said. "I'm taking him trick-or-treating in the stroller so he can see all the children. You can't start early enough with the little ones. I want him to be a part of everything and that includes Halloween." Dory nodded agreeably. Griff was certainly going to be surprised when he came home this evening and saw her outdoor arrangement. She was handy and creative, as Lily pointed out. "You've changed since you got here," Lily smiled as she stuffed straw arms into a plaid shirt.

"How so?" Dory asked.

"When you first arrived you were New York City from the top of your head to the tip of your toes. You were like Sylvia would like to be but isn't. Do you know what I mean? You had the clothes, the right hairstyle; by the way, would you like me to trim your hair? I'm real good at it. I always cut Rick's hair."

"Sure." She giggled to herself. She wondered what her stylist at Vidal Sassoon would say if he could see Lily "trimming" her hair.

"Anyway, as I was saying, now you're just like everyone else. You cook, you clean, you go to school, and you've come out of your shell. I bet Griff is happy with all you've been doing."

Dory frowned. Was Griff happy with the things she had done? Or was he tolerating her? She wasn't sure. He seemed to have changed too. The pressures of the new clinic and all, she told herself. He never seemed to want to go out unless it was to someone's house. Money, she told herself. It always came down to money. She hated to see the look of concern on Griff's face when he made out the bills. Perhaps she should have offered some of her money. Next month, she told herself. After all, she was buying the groceries and she had paid for all the decorating. Surely he didn't expect more. He seemed drawn and tense these days. And twice a day he quizzed her about school and how she was doing. She found to her chagrin that she was beginning to lie, telling him she went to class when she stayed home to trim the plants and feed and water them. Or just to sit and read *Redbook* all by herself. She always felt guilty when she did something like that and then would outdo herself cooking a gastronomical feast for Griff.

"Is he?" Lily prodded.

"Is he what?" Dory asked, coming out of her reverie.

"Is he happy with the way you've taken over and turned that house into a home?"

"I think so. Griff doesn't say much. Sometimes it's hard to tell, and you know all three of the guys are up tight with the clinic. He comes home some nights and falls into bed exhausted.

But I think he's happy." Dory spoke with more confidence than she felt.

"Well, I know one thing for certain. Rick says Griff's so proud of you sometimes he gets on his nerves the way he talks about you."

"Rick said that?" Dory's eyes glowed like moonbeams at the words.

"That's what it's all about, Dory," Lily said softly. "Taking pride in one another's accomplishments. Griff is so pleased that you're going to school and that one day you'll hold your doctorate. He brags about you to John, too. Sylvia told me just the other day. By the way, what's wrong with her? She seemed out of sorts." Dory shrugged. She didn't want to get into a discussion of Sylvia.

Lily finished the torso of her scarecrow and watched as Dory followed her instructions. She admitted to herself that she hadn't liked Dory Faraday when she met her for the first time. She felt responsible for Dory's transformation, as she called it. She didn't feel at all guilty about subtly persuading Dory that her own lifestyle was far superior to Sylvia's gypsy, freewheeling attitude. Her patience had been rewarded; Dory had become domesticated. Yes, she liked Dory Faraday much better now, and she would like her even more if only she wouldn't withdraw at times into her own secret world. Meanwhile she would stand by and be the good friend that Dory needed. Who knows, she mused to herself, I may even talk her into marriage.

"I'm done, what do you think?" Dory asked as she propped her straw man next to Lily's.

"Perfect," Lily said as if she were talking to her prize pupil. "I want you to call me after Griff sees it and tell me what he says. Promise now," she said, wagging her finger in the air.

"Okay. I've got to run now. I'm going to make that apple pie you gave me the recipe for. I bought the apples at the stand where you told me to go. While it's baking I have some notes to transcribe. By the way, I took some cuttings from my plants. If you want them, you can stop by tomorrow. I'll make lunch this time.''

"Wonderful. Now don't forget to use the large pumpkin instead of the small one. By the way, what are you and Griff doing for Thanksgiving?''

"I'm not sure. He hasn't mentioned anything.''

"Rick and I would love to have you. We make a real big deal over the holidays. I'm having twenty people. We'd love it if you'd come,'' she repeated.

"I'll speak to Griff. If he's agreeable, what can I bring?''

"Pies,'' Lily said promptly. "Pumpkin, of course, and several of the apple quince I showed you how to make. A pecan one would be nice too, just to be different.''

Dory bent down to dangle her fingers at the baby and then looked around. Lily's house was screamingly neat. She frowned. Something should be out of place. Some piece of lint on the carpet, something.

All the way back to the town house she thought about Lily and her neat house and about Sylvia who lived like the Queen of the Gypsies. The thoughts did nothing for her tense mood. She was getting a headache. She was getting a lot of headaches lately. And she had gained seven pounds. Seven pounds in all the wrong places. Griff had jabbed at her playfully and mentioned it. Womanly. She looked womanly. She banished the word matronly from her mind.

Griff sat in the clinic offices, a small puppy in his lap. He fondled the silky ears and knew he should put the little dog back in its cage. He should be doing a lot of things, like getting ready to go home. He glanced at his watch. It was after seven. He should have left an hour ago. There was no pressing business. Rick had seen to everything in the office and clinic before he left at five-thirty. One thing about Rick, hell or high water, he left at five-thirty on the dot. He had a family and regular hours were a must. Sit-down dinner was at six-fifteen. By keeping regular hours he had a good thirty minutes to play and cuddle with his son. His family would always come first. He had been honest, laid it on the line with Griff and John, before he signed his share of the partnership.

Griff stared at the puppy, wondering what Dory was making for dinner. Six-course dinners were beginning to take their toll on his waistline and hers as well. Maybe a few hours of racquetball would do him some good. He'd call Dory and tell her he had to work late. Homemaker Dory would never understand that he would rather play racquetball than be with her. And it wasn't true. He just wanted some time for himself, time to work off some hostility. God, now why had that word cropped up? What in hell did he have to feel hostile about? Nothing. Not a damn thing. That wasn't exactly true either. His bank balance was precariously low. He was living like a prince, or maybe a king, due to Dory's intense efforts, so he really shouldn't complain, but he was going to have to. The rent and utilities were draining him. When the heat was turned on his bill would triple. Dory's second-quarter tuition would be due, the holidays were around the corner, and he needed some new clothes. A long talk with Dory was called for. If not tonight, then by the weekend.

Still, he didn't carry the puppy to its cage. This quiet time to himself was a balm. Everyone needed some space. When two people lived together they had a tendency to smother one another. That was it, he felt smothered. How it happened, how it got a foothold, he had no idea. Dory really was Superwoman. She went to class, worked on her papers at night, cooked, cleaned, and still managed to have a social life with Sylvia and Lily. If that was the case then why did he feel smothered? Was there such a thing as one person being too good to another? He loved her. God, how he loved her. If he searched the world over he could never find anyone he could love more. Then why the dissatisfaction? Why was he dragging his feet about going home? Why did he want to play racquetball? Why? Why? Maybe he needed a drink. He should call Dory. He really should.

The black and white puppy yipped its displeasure when he was put back in the cage. "It's a cold, hard world out here, little guy. Be thankful you have a place to sleep," Griff said softly as he shut the cage and turned off all but the night lights.

Griff drove past the racquetball club and then made a U-turn and drove back. Cal Williams's car was in the lot; there was no mistaking the ruby-red Ferarri. Cal could really give him a workout. He knew he should call Dory. Instead, he walked by the phone booth without a second glance.

When Griff walked into the kitchen a little after ten, he expected Dory to be fighting mad because her dinner was ruined. Instead, she smiled, laid aside the notes she was transcribing. He saw his dinner plate and silverware. "It'll only take a minute to warm in the microwave. Go along and take your shower. Would you like a drink?"

"Not really. How about a diet soda?"

Dory frowned. "I don't think we have any. Sylvia had the last bottle yesterday. How about some coffee or beer?"

"Ice water. I have to start watching my weight. All this rich food is going straight to my waist. That Sylvia really does watch her figure, doesn't she?" he asked, looking pointedly at Dory.

"Yes, she does. But, Griff, she's like a stringy hen."

"I never noticed," he said blandly. "I'm not all that hungry, so don't make much for me." He opted for the truth. "I played racquetball and picked up a hot dog with Cal Williams."

"Oh, is that where you were. I thought you were working late. Why didn't you call me? I would have waited dinner."

Now. Now the fireworks would start. Instead, Dory grinned. "Who won?"

"He did. He's in shape. He noticed the weight I put on and ribbed me all night. Cut down, Dory, forget the pies and bread and give me salads and chicken." His tone was cooler and more curt than he intended. Dory's face fell. She looked guilty and frightened. God, why would she look *frightened?* "Hey, it's not the end of the world. I've always been weight conscious, you know that. You used to be too. Somewhere, somehow, we've gotten off the track. Let's get back on before we get to the point where it's hard to take the pounds

103

off." He watched carefully for her reaction. There was none. She moved away from the stove and stared at him for a minute.

"I can fix you some chicken if you want. It won't take long."

"No. Just some salad. In fact, I don't even want salad. I feel bad that you cooked all this food." *And* spent all this money, he thought.

"It's no problem. If you're sure you don't want anything, I'll get back to my work."

Goddamn it, Griff thought as the needle-sharp spray attacked him. She made him feel guilty. Then he grinned. A tiff. They were having a tiff and what fun it would be to make up.

Dory was usually the first one in bed, her arms and body waiting for him. Tonight, she elected to stay in the kitchen to work. Christ, was she going to start holding him off when something didn't set right with her? He hated the thought. Hated the impulse that came over him to run downstairs and take her in his arms. Hated the thought that he would even go so far as eating the food he didn't want. He gave the pillow a vicious punch and then another. He rolled over and tried to sleep. He was still wide awake at three o'clock when Dory crept into bed. She lay so far to the edge he thought she would fall out of bed if she moved. He wanted to gather her in his arms and make love to her. Her stiff body told him she might agree but it would be on her terms. There was no giving in her this evening. Jesus. Women! He closed his eyes and eventually slept.

Warm tears soaked into the satiny pillowcase. What did I do, she cried silently. And he never noticed the scarecrow leaning crookedly against the front door.

Chapter Seven

It was raining hard the next morning when Dory woke. She crawled from bed and padded down to the kitchen. She put coffee on to perk and pulled out the toaster. If Griff didn't want her homemade cinnamon rolls then he could have dry toast with his coffee. She would eat the rolls herself and smear butter all over them. It wasn't an easy task to make cinnamon rolls from scratch and she refused to waste them.

The phone rang. It was Lily. "I can't possibly come to lunch today," she apologized. "I can't take the baby out in this weather and the morning news says this is going to keep on for the whole day."

Dory voiced her disappointment, but she felt secretly relieved. Lunch with Lily might have been nice, but there were other things that needed doing today, and at least she wouldn't have to rush home from the university to prepare a sumptuous lunch straight out of the pages of *Woman's Day*.

Griff walked into the kitchen. He assessed the situation of Dory sitting at the table lathing butter on the cinnamon roll and kissed her soundly. "Oh, they look delicious. I'll have two with lots of butter."

"No, you won't. You're having dry toast with your coffee. I'm having the rolls." She smiled to take the sting out of her words. "How did you sleep last night?"

"Fine," Griff lied. Damn, he really wanted the cinnamon rolls. "How about you?"

"Fine," Dory lied in return.

Griff gulped his coffee and reached for the toast. "I think I'll eat this on the way to the clinic. See you this evening. Remember, it's my late night tonight. Do you have classes today?"

"One at ten and another at twelve. I should be home by one at the latest," Dory replied, biting into the warm bun.

The minute the door closed behind Griff, Dory tossed the rolls into the trash. She watched the driving rain as she sipped her coffee. There was no way she was driving out to Georgetown in this weather. This was the kind of day you cleaned out closets or baked cookies. But her closets were neat, and if Griff was on a diet, that left schoolwork or a book to be read.

She admitted she loved to snuggle in and putter around. A whole, entire day to snuggle and putter. Maybe she would call Katy and Pixie and see how they were doing on the article for *Soiree*. After she made the bed, that is, and cleaned the bathroom and rinsed the dishes and coffee pot. Then she would relax with a fresh pot of coffee and make her calls. Maybe it was time to see about the profiles. Katy was certain to ask how that was going and she didn't want to lie. On the other hand, she could do what all the other freelancers did, say she was *on top of it*. If the rain stopped, she could take a trip to Ollie's Trolley and see if the senator showed up. But that meant she would have to get dressed and schlepp out in the puddles. A girl could ruin her shoes doing something like that. Perhaps today wasn't the day to think about calling Katy or Pixie. Her eye went to the calendar by the phone. It was almost time to call Lizzie. Dory counted the large red X's and groaned. Where *had* the time gone?

Gay little notes penned by the office staff and Katy had been arriving with regularity these past weeks. For some reason they frightened her. She always tore up the notes and then was nervous and edgy for the rest of the day.

There was no point in calling Pixie either. Pixie would chatter on and on about what a wonderful time she was having as the star of a *Soiree* story. She really didn't want to hear about it.

You don't want to go to school; you don't want to get in touch with the senator; you don't want to call your friends; what *do* you want? A tired voice within her answered: "God, I wish I knew." Lately, she couldn't seem to make even the smallest decision about herself. She knew she should be hitting the books, attending the lectures, taking notes. She knew she should go on a diet and take off at least eight pounds. The number made her blink in awe. Eight pounds!

Maybe she should call Sylvia and ask her to go shopping. It was time to think about Thanksgiving decorations, and while she was at it, she could pick up some new knickknacks for Griff's den. The crystal unicorn he had admired in Neiman-Marcus.

I'll buy you a gift, a bribe if you will, and you be nice to me. Don't notice me for my lack of direction. Don't make me feel frightened. Don't ever do that to me again, Griff, she pleaded silently.

Something was wrong.

What?

Who to believe?

Sylvia? "Spend. Enjoy. Reach out, take it. Go for it."

Lily? "Snuggle in. Let's cook, bake and decorate. Be creative in your home. Forget independence. Forget the outside world, it's cold and cruel. Let Griff worry about it all."

Hide!

School?

It's hard. Work, work, work. Headaches. Nervous indigestion. Notes, always notes. More notes.

Take off those eight pounds. *Now.* Before it's too late.

Career. Once it was the most important thing in life. B.G. Before Griff. Griff said he understood. Everyone needed a hiatus.

Hide!

Hide from Katy, from Pixie, from the unseen senator, from Lizzie.

David Harlow!!!

The red X's on the calendar seemed to run together.

Was this the way it was supposed to be?

Aunt Pixie would tell her to clean up her act and straighten up and fly right. What did Pix know? She lived in a wine bottle.

Something was wrong. Was Griff falling out of love with her?

Was she falling out of love with Griff?

Never!

David Harlow!

The red X's.

Decisions.

Challenges.

Hide. For God's sake hide!

Griff.

Dory looked around, unseeing. Her heart was fluttering wildly. She could call Griff and Griff would make it better. Whatever it was.

No!

I can take care of myself. I have for years. I don't need anyone to take care of me.

Givvve meee aaa breaaakkk, the inner voice chided. If that's true, why are you sitting here doing nothing? A non contributor.

The phone rang. Dory glared at it as if it were the enemy.

Dory didn't realize how cautious her voice sounded till she heard Griff asking her who she was trying to evade.

"No one. Why would you say such a thing?" Dory asked fretfully.

"Dory, I hate to bring this up, especially on the phone, but right now I don't have any other choice. The clinic needs a new centrifuge. If I put in my share, which I intend to do, my personal account is going to hit rock bottom. Now, we both agreed when we signed the lease for the town house that you were going to help with the finances. I didn't like it then and I still don't like it. You convinced me that it was the right move and I went along with it. The rent and the utilities are due in five days. I have a car payment to make and some payments on my charge accounts. If we can't swing the payments, then we're going to have to try and break the lease and move some place cheaper. I told you that I wouldn't be taking a salary for the first six months and things were going to be lean. I'm sorry, Dory.''

"But, Griff, I've been buying all the food and I did pay for all the extras, the chair for your den and the drapes and plants,'' Dory said in a shocked voice.

"Those were things we didn't need, Dory. I'm talking about the essentials. Didn't you hear what I just said? Once I pay this month's rent and pay my bills, I'm virtually wiped out. How would it look to John and Rick if I went back on my word and asked for an advance? I won't do it, Dory. I want you to think about this today, and we'll talk this evening when I get home. Dory, are you listening to me?''

"Yes, I am. And I'm shocked. You never told me your bank account was so low. I thought you had . . . what I mean is, I expected . . . oh, I don't know what I mean,'' Dory fretted. She didn't like this conversation. She didn't like it at all. As a matter of fact, she hated this conversation.

When she hung up the phone she swallowed hard. He was supposed to be taking care of her, providing for her. God, what if she had married him? If she had married him, would he have said the same thing to her? Griff wanted money from her. How cool and detached his voice was. How impersonal. How goddamn impersonal.

She had spent at least three thousand dollars. Maybe more. What more did he want? Hadn't she knocked herself out making the town house a home to be proud of? Hadn't she forsaken all else to make Griff a comfortable place to live? She had neglected school, her freelance work, *everything*, to be what Griff wanted. Now, it wasn't enough. He wanted more. He wanted her share. Did he have any idea how expensive food was? Did he think she liked running to the damn supermarket every two days? Did he think she liked all this hausfrau work? Did he think she liked cooking and doing dishes? God, where was the time for herself? And the gas, who did he think paid for the fuel for the gas-guzzling station wagon? Some magical gnome who had an unlimited supply of money?

It wasn't supposed to be like this.

"How *was* it supposed to be?" The inner voice asked petulantly.

Dory sputtered. "Certainly not like this," she said to the empty kitchen.

Rain beat against the kitchen windows, beating a tattoo as fast as her heart was beating. Her share.

She felt like throwing a fit. Anger, hot and scorching, coursed through her, the first honest emotion she had felt since moving into the town house. She stormed about the kitchen, beating at the appliances with her bare fists. Cups and saucers were swept willy-nilly from the table onto the floor. She kicked out at them. Her share! What was her share? Was it making a home? Doing the cooking? The shopping? Thinking of his every need? His every whim? He accused her of not pulling her share!

Ignoring the mess, she raced up the stairs and pulled her suitcases out of the closet.

Run.

Hide.

Leave.

Go where?

Do what?

Her share!

Admit defeat!

Admit to being worthless!

Her share!

Griff's disappointment in her!

It wasn't supposed to be like this. Tears of self pity rolled down her cheeks. She continued to sit on the edge of the bed, staring at her open suitcase. This was silly, childish. If she were Griff's wife, the suitcase wouldn't be on the bed. She wouldn't have thought of leaving. Theirs would be a marriage, not a partnership that shared expenses.

Marriage. Was that her choice? Was that little piece of paper the difference between a commitment and a financial arrangement? A man protected and took care of and supported his wife. With his lover he had every right to expect her to pay her share.

Dory admitted it wasn't the money. Money was only incidental. What hurt was discovering that all she had done, all she had accomplished in making a real home for the two of them was unappreciated. The decorations, the drapes, the plants . . . on and on she could add to the list . . . and it wasn't appreciated. The bills were due. She could give him the damn money, that didn't matter. It was knowing that all she had done was meaningless. Griff preferred to deal in hard facts and figures and remind her of broken promises.

The rain continued to beat its cacophony against the windows. At least they would get a good washing, she thought inanely.

The ringing phone demanded her attention. She ignored it.

Anger fought to the surface and she squelched it. More self-pity. Her world was falling apart. Nothing was the way she thought it would be. Not Griff. Not even herself. Nothing.

An inner voice warned her against taking rash action. "Slow and easy," it told her. "Think. You can handle this. Make a decision and stick to it. Do something, for God's sake! Anything, just do it!"

The phone shrilled a second time. "Hello," she snapped into the receiver.

"Dory, is that you?" the voice on the other end of the phone queried hesitantly.

"Katy!" Dory squealed. "My God, Katy, is it really you? I'm so glad you called. What are you doing? What's going on at *Soiree*? Tell me everything. How are all the girls? What's going on with the layout? How did Pixie do? Did the girls like her? Tell me the truth. I want to know everything. How's the weather in the city? Smoggy, I bet. How's your husband and the cat? Don't leave a thing out. You're calling on the WATS line, aren't you? Shoot," Dory said breathlessly.

"Is it that bad?" Katy asked.

"Yeah. Now tell me everything."

"Okay but first I called you with a few problems. I hope you don't mind. Let's get them out of the way first and then we can gossip."

"Hit me."

Fifteen minutes later Katy grumbled. "God, it was so simple. I should have been able to figure all of this out myself. I guess that's why you're you and I'm me. I'm telling you, Dory, you did this magazine a favor when you sent us your aunt. The place hasn't been the same since. She's got Harlow eating right out of her hand. I think she's lusting after him and making no bones about it. She's got to be the horniest woman I ever came across." There was open awe and admiration in Katy's voice when she continued. "And she isn't faking it either. Another thing I wanted to tell you. I sent some layout copy to you for your approval. Harlow says it doesn't go until you initial it. I thought that was swell. Do you agree?"

"Harlow said that? You aren't kidding me, are you?" She was feeling better and better by the minute.

"No way. He said this was yours and you have to pass final approval and he didn't care if you were residing in Nome, Alaska."

"Super," Dory said. Compliments from on high were so rare that when they did fall one had to be ready to catch and appreciate them.

"Pixie hosted a dinner party at the Sign of the Dove for all the crew and everyone from *Soiree* who wanted to attend. I might add that she had one hundred percent attendance. She's a trip. Harlow was so impressed with the check I thought he was going to pass out. I left at two-thirty and the girls were telling me that the management stayed open till four to accommodate Pixie. I'm telling you, this place is like a morgue now that she's gone."

Dory laughed. Good old Pixie. She really did things up right and then tied a big red bow on them. She did leave her mark. "Tell me, what's with Lizzie?"

"Things are going great. She's delirious. She's really counting on you, Dory."

"I know. I'm working on it, Katy. Don't crowd me, okay?"

"Wouldn't think of it. Eileen is pregnant and is taking a

leave of absence. Sandy is having a torrid romance with our new art director and loving every minute of it. Jamie is buying a cottage in the country and is going to renovate it weekends by herself.''

"With those three-inch-long fingernails?" Dory laughed.

"That's what I said. She said they were false and she can remove them at will. It'll give her something to do on the train ride back to the city on Sunday nights."

"How's your husband and the cat?"

"In the order of importance. Goliath is fine. Eats two containers of Tender Vittles a day. He's getting so fat he can't jump up on the bed anymore. As for my other half. What could be new? Let's face it, the honeymoon has been over for a long time. I really hate the way he does the laundry. One week everything is pink, the next week, everything is blue. He refuses to separate."

Dory doubled over laughing. Katy was so good for her. God, how she missed everyone. "What else?"

"Well, one day this week a whole truckload of plants arrived and no one knows where or who they came from. No one remembers the name of the delivery company. When I tell you plants I mean plants. Wait till you see your office. The place is a damn jungle. I think Pixie sent them. Because. . . ." Katy strung out her words, "she made a remark that she looked best among green things. At the time I didn't get it but I do now. She wanted to go *à la naturelle* with assorted flora and fauna. We covered her up a little and used some rental plants. Anyway, the place is a jungle. I have to pay someone overtime just to water them and spritz them every day."

There was a pause. Dory was too overcome to say anything.

"We miss you, Dory. All the girls said to give you their regards."

"I miss you all too. Say hello for me. And, Katy, thanks for calling."

"Any time. Thank you for helping me out. I was going crazy with all that stuff. You make it sound so simple. Sometimes I wish I were you."

"No you don't," Dory said softly. "Don't ever wish that. Be sure you say hello to everyone."

"I wish you'd come in and do it yourself," Katy grumbled as she hung up the phone.

Damn it, she did miss all of them. She really did. The brief workout on the phone was exactly what she needed. But was it what she wanted?

Dory lay back on the bed and let her mind go blank. Within seconds she was asleep.

Chapter Eight

D ORY WOKE UP AN HOUR LATER FEELING LITTLE BETTER THAN when she had escaped into sleep. Her drowsiness gave way to self-pity when her eyes fell on the open suitcase at the foot of the bed. Groggily, she inched her way to the bottom of the bed and slammed the suitcase shut. The sound was almost terminal in the silent room. She fell back against the warm nest of the silken comforter, her eyes brimming with unshed tears. In some inexplicable way she was feeling threatened. Frightened. Afraid. And she realized that instead of trying to understand the reasons, she was trying to escape her roiling emotions. But if she couldn't feel safe here, in her home and Griff's, where would she be safe? If she couldn't handle her own emotions, she couldn't handle anything. So much for her brief high on Katy's phone call.

Impatient with herself, Dory slid from the bed. Perhaps she should give more thought to marrying Griff. It wouldn't be hard to manipulate him . . . What was she thinking of? Manipulate! Certainly Griff still wanted to marry her; he had asked her to be his wife months ago—before coming to Washington. If anything, he wanted her to marry him more than ever! She was the one with the problem, the indecision! Had she actually thought of manipulating him into marriage? She was aghast. She needed to get her head together. Needed to talk to someone.

She could call Lily. Lily was safe. Safe in her role as

mother and as wife. Lily knew exactly what she wanted. And, she had her own little built-in insurance policy—the baby. Lily was as safe as if she were wrapped in a silken cocoon. There were no pressures on Lily to succeed. Lily never had to worry about failing. Lily was safe and Dory could be safe too. If she married Griff, she wouldn't be failing; she would just be quitting the game. There was no dishonor in that. Or was there? God, she just didn't know any more.

She lugged the Gucci suitcase back to the closet. Angrily, she kicked at the red and green strip on its side. If she took it to the flea market, she could sell it and get enough money to buy groceries or maybe even pay the electric bill. Would anyone at a flea market even know what a Gucci suitcase was? How pleased she'd been the day she had bought it, along with its matching weekend bag. She had wanted it, so she had bought it, using over two weeks' salary to pay for it. She hadn't even given the price a second thought. It was enough to know that she had earned the money and could spend it as she saw fit. There was nothing wrong with wanting things. Permission wasn't required to buy it. God, how she hated the damn thing. On Saturday she would sell both the pieces. Lily would approve. Sylvia . . . Sylvia would sneer and ask her what she planned on packing her clothes in . . . a shopping bag? Sylvia had a complete set of Louis Vuitton.

November turned into a depressing month. All the glorious colors of autumn were long gone. The days turned cold and rain seemed to be a daily occurrence. Dory dreaded the coming of winter with the biting wind and icy sleet almost as much as she dreaded Griff's end-of-the-month lectures on spending.

Thanksgiving passed as just another day except for dinner at Lily's house. She had dutifully baked her pies and mashed the turnips as requested. She vowed to eat sparingly and then said the hell with it and ate as much as everyone else.

The digital scale in the mulberry bathroom said she was

now eleven pounds over her normal weight. Just one pound over ten. Only three pounds over eight. Referred to in that manner, it didn't seem so ominous.

And always, no matter what she did, no matter how she tried to avoid contact with the kitchen calendar, she found her eyes clicking off the red X's. It was now dangerously close to the countdown when she would have to make the call to Lizzie.

Georgetown was a farce. She cut more classes than she attended. When she did do the reading, she couldn't remember any of it afterward. Oh, she made a pretense of poring over books and compiling long lists of notes. More often than not they were household lists and grocery lists. Griff never seemed to notice. He tiptoed around the kitchen if he saw her bent over her books and notebooks.

For some reason, Dory felt betrayed. Or was she the betrayer?

December made its entrance with a heavy snowfall. The mounds of white stuff depressed Dory. It wasn't till Lily called and suggested a trip to the evergreen farm to pick and chop their own Christmas trees that her spirits perked up. They bundled little Ricky into an apple-red snowsuit and started off. First, they stopped by Sylvia's house to see if she wanted to accompany them.

"Darlings, no one in her right mind chops down Christmas trees. It's . . . it's decadent. Your feet will get wet in all that . . . that snow. You'll catch cold and your hands will get chapped. Ridiculous! And, what about that child? What if he needs to nurse? I think you're out of your mind, Lily. Call Sears Roebuck and have them deliver an artificial tree. They even come trimmed."

Lily grinned. "This is Ricky's first Christmas and it would be sacrilege to have a plastic tree. Do you want us to bring you back some evergreens for trimming?"

"And mess up the house? No, thank you!"

"I wonder how she'd notice a few pine needles." Lily continued to giggle.

Dory sat contentedly with the baby in her lap. He was cute

even if he slobbered all over everything, even if his shrill sounds made Dory wince. Motherhood. She inched the baby farther to her knees and stared at him, lost in thought. They did require a lot of work. Everyone wasn't cut out for parenting. Lily was the perfect mother who should have a houseful of kids to run after. Bottles and diapers and laundry. Baby-sitters and mashed food. She hated the idea. Still . . . maybe she could learn to adjust. Having one's own baby would certainly be different from holding someone else's. Your own flesh and blood. Griff's blood and her flesh. Her labor, her agony. Her sweat. Her stitches. Long and careful thought would be required before she made a decision.

Lily had borrowed the clinic van so she and Dory could bring back their Christmas trees. Now, fingers frozen and toes just beginning to warm from the van's heater, they were on their way home. Two trees and bundles of green boughs filled the van with fresh natural scent. Little Ricky sat plac-idly on Dory's lap, drooling onto the front of his Winnie-the-Pooh snowsuit. His sweet, warm head lolled against her as he nodded off to sleep.

"Lily, little Ricky is falling asleep and I know it's not his nap time. The cold air must have knocked him out. Do you want me to keep him awake so he'll sleep when you get him home?" After numerous days spent with Lily and her baby Dory was becoming quite familiar with their schedules and the way Lily liked to do things.

"Let him sleep if he wants." Lily concentrated on the road. "It really doesn't make much difference. Rick won't be coming home till late."

Dory raised her brows, looking at Lily quizzically. What had happened since they left the evergreen farm? Why did Lily seem so despondent? Or was it her own brand of anger? "I suppose you're dissatisfied when Rick needs to stay late at the clinic."

"That's a funny word, Dory. Dissatisfied? Don't you mean disappointed?"

Dory wasn't used to having Lily bring her up short. "Yes . . . yes, I suppose I do. Disappointed, then?"

Lily bit her lip, her pink, wind-stung cheeks making her chestnut hair seem more vivid. "I am disappointed in a lot of things." This she said quietly, almost solemnly, and Dory wondered if there was trouble in Lily's paradise. But Lily didn't seem to want to talk about it, and Dory was glad. She didn't want to hear that Lily wasn't safe. Out of the blue, Lily asked a question.

"Have you met the new receptionist-secretary at the clinic yet? I've been meaning to bring in one of my coffee cakes and get down there to decorate for Christmas. You know, just to bring the holiday spirit into the outer office. Little Rick's pediatrician has these cute little felt angels hanging all around the waiting room. I don't know who made them, probably his wife."

Dory was having difficulty following Lily's train of thought. Did she want to talk about Ginny, the new receptionist, or did she want to talk about decorating the office? The latter seemed safer. "If you want we could buy some of those Hallmark paper decorations, and I'll go down there with you to put them up. We could go when surgery is scheduled so the waiting room will be empty."

Lily nodded, concentrating on the road. "Well, have you? Have you met this girl they've hired?"

"No, but I've spoken to her on the phone. She seems very nice . . . I guess," she added when she saw Lily's features stiffen.

"When the baby was born Rick promised he wouldn't work past office hours," Lily complained. "I even heard him tell Griff and John myself. This will be the second night this week he's staying late."

"Do you want me to say something to Griff? Perhaps he and John don't understand how important your evenings are."

"No, Dory, don't say anything. I . . . I wouldn't want Rick to know I'm being such a baby just because he had to work late a few nights." Her mouth was drawn into a thin line as though she were biting back what she really wanted to talk about. "Hey!" She tried for forced brightness. "There's the stand where they sell the best apple cider outside of New

York State! You remember, Dory, I served it for Thanksgiving and everyone loved it. Let's stop."

"Sure. I love cider. I'll stay here with the baby."

While Lily bought the cider, Dory sat holding little Rick. He felt warm and cuddly as she shifted him to a more comfortable position. Something was wrong with Lily. She was trying too hard. There were times, like right now, when Lily seemed almost frantic and just a shade too enthusiastic about her recipes and her decorating, not to mention her "happy, happy" home life. She seemed to be working overtime to convince herself that everything was wonderful. Or was she trying to convince Dory? Poor Lily, she was so vulnerable. How, Dory wondered, was it so possible for a woman to become so locked into family and home? She supposed she could question Lily, but Lily would say only what she wanted Dory to know, no more and no less. She would wear a stricken look and tears would come to her eyes. No, it was better not to ask questions of Lily. If Lily had a problem she would have to be the one to bring it up.

"Well what's it going to be, are we going to get the decorations for the office or not?" Dory asked as she sipped at her apple cider.

It wasn't Dory's imagination. Lily's eyes took on a frightened look as she contemplated her answer. "No, I don't think so. When I mentioned it to Rick he didn't seem too interested. He said Ginny would do the decorating."

"But I thought you said . . ." Dory clamped her mouth shut at Lily's stricken face.

"I know what I said. The truth is, I wanted an excuse to go to the office to take a look at Ginny. Sylvia said she's stunning. If Sylvia says she's stunning that means she looks like Cheryl Tiegs."

"Sylvia exaggerates a great deal. So what if she does look like a model? What does that have to do with you?" Dory asked softly.

Lily turned to face Dory. "It has a great deal to do with me. It happened once before. I told you Rick was going to be late; this is the second time this week. That's the way it started the last time. Beautiful receptionist, handsome young doctor. Sylvia took it on herself to tell me about it. She also took it upon herself to have John fire the girl. Her name was Maxine. I never told Rick I knew. He was different for a while but he straightened out. That's why I decided to have the baby. I was so sure it would bring us closer together. I was so sure if I had a baby things would go back to the way they were before. I keep a spotless house, I cook wonderful meals. Little Rick is a delight to both Rick and me. I do everything a good wife is supposed to do. I think I'm reasonably good in bed. Rick certainly never complained. Everyone who comes to the house compliments Rick on what a wonderful wife and mother I am.'' Tears filled Lily's eyes as she stared at Dory. ''If I'm such a wonderful wife and mother why does Rick have to look somewhere else? And he's looking. It's the same old pattern.''

Dory stared at her friend, aware of the contented baby in her arms. My God, Lily had actually had a baby to try and solve her problems. How awful for Lily. Playing Mother Earth wasn't her answer. Poor Lily. Men were such bastards. How could Rick do this to her? ''Lily, I don't know. I just don't know. I assumed that everything was all right between you and Rick. You aren't sure of anything. You think he's doing something, but you aren't sure. Why don't you talk to him, get it out in the open? Tell him you know about the first time. It may not be true this time. Give him a chance.''

Lily was appalled at the suggestion. ''I could never do that!''

''Why not? Once the air is cleared you can go on from there. I know you love Rick deeply. Make a fresh start.''

''I can't do it. I simply can't do it.''

''What are you going to do, have another baby to make it come right for you? Are you going to depend on Sylvia to find out about this one so she can tell John to fire Ginny? You can't rely on babies to solve your problems. You have to work them out yourself, and silent suffering isn't the answer.''

''Maybe not, but that's the way it has to be for now,'' Lily said in a cheerful voice. ''I'm so glad we stopped for the

cider. Rick likes to drink it in front of the fireplace before we
go to bed. He'll be so pleased that I got it.''

Dory had to physically shake her head to clear it. How
could Lily turn on and off like that? From long practice she
answered herself: Safe, secure Lily was frightened. Safe,
secure Lily who thought she had Rick to support her and love
her and give meaning to her life. If Lily could be insecure,
where did that leave Dory?

When Dory arrived home from the evergreen farm she
found a note from Griff on the kitchen table telling her he
wouldn't be home that night and not to expect him until late
the following evening. Something about a horse and a colt
that was refusing to nurse. Dory hadn't realized she had been
holding her breath till a long sigh escaped her with a loud
swoosh. She would certainly have more than enough time to
decorate the house with boughs of greenery. She was removing her boots when the phone rang. Kicking off one stout
rubber boot, she hopped to the phone and caught it on the
second ring. She fully expected to hear Sylvia's voice demanding to know if she was sneezing yet or had a fever. The
breathless, squeaky voice left no doubt who was on the other
end of the phone. It was Aunt Pixie. Pixie never believed in
the social amenities. She got right to the point.

"I'm at the damn airport. Will you kindly tell me how in
the living hell I get to the boonies where you live?"

"You're early, aren't you?"

"Only by two weeks. Will it be a problem? If it is, you're
stuck with me regardless. Just give me directions. The cab
driver hasn't been born yet that I'd trust.''

Dory issued brief, concise instructions that she knew Pixie
would never remember. "I'll have a hot toddy waiting.
Shouldn't take you more than twenty minutes. You'll beat
traffic by at least an hour.''

"Never mind the toddy. I don't want any garbage clouding
up my drink. You just get the bottle out and make sure you
have a long-stemmed glass.''

Dory laughed. "You haven't changed a bit. I'm dying to
see you. Hurry and hang up and get here so we can talk.''

Forty-five minutes later a whirlwind with six suitcases and a trunk sailed through Dory's kitchen. "I take it you're staying awhile," Dory grinned.

"Three days. I'm on my way to Hong Kong," Pixie said as she uncapped the squat bottle of scotch. She poured the amber liquid into a long-stemmed glass and drank it neat. "What do you say we get sloshed?" she said, tilting the bottle a second time.

"Sounds good to me," Dory agreed, getting out a glass for herself.

Pixie tossed her sable coat over the kitchen chair and Dory hugged her enthusiastically. "Watch the wig, watch the wig!" Pixie squeaked as she tried to adjust the precarious pile of red-gold curls.

"Oh, God, Pix, I forgot. Sorry. You look . . .great."

"I know, I know. A real pity you and I are the only ones who think so. People actually turn around and stare at me and it's not always with admiration." She sipped her scotch approvingly. "Now that I've taken the edge off a little we can do some serious drinking. All they served on that miserable flight was Diet Pepsi. Diet Pepsi. I told that stewardess what I thought of that, let me tell you. All that saccharin. My God! A body isn't safe anywhere any more. By the way, you look like something the cat dragged in, took a second look and then dragged back out. What'd you do, sneak back in when he wasn't looking?"

"Thanks," Dory said dryly. She sipped at her drink.

Pixie fumbled in her handbag and eventually found a pair of granny glasses. She propped them on the end of her nose and stared at Dory. Her mouth dropped open as she regarded her favorite niece. Her only niece. "Pudgy. God, I envy women who have the guts to be pudgy. I have to work at staying this thin," she said proudly as she stuck out a long, skinny leg clad in a white leather boot. Dory wouldn't have been surprised to see a pom-pom attached to the top.

"I know you do," Dory agreed as she watched the glass tilt again. There was no stopping Pixie. She drank like a fish and had no intention of stopping. She also smoked incessantly.

123

"What time will *Grit* be home. I'm anxious to see him. I'm sorry I won't be able to spend Christmas with you two but I got this offer"—her voice dropped to a hushed whisper—"from this gentleman I've been corresponding with and he invited me to come to Hong Kong for a visit. He makes shoes. Hand-made shoes. He's Chinese, Japanese, one of those nationalities. He said he has western eyes. Shoes. Imagine, Dory. If he works out, we can get all our shoes for nothing. Just tell me what you want. Do you still have some kind of fixation about shoes. Or maybe it's a fetish."

Dory giggled. It was just like Pixie to go traipsing halfway around the world in the hopes of getting something free. It wasn't so much the shoes as a man that Pixie hoped to get.

"I'll be seventy-two next year. It's time I thought about settling down. I always liked Hong Kong. I can see me settling down over there. I'll get manicures and pedicures. Those people love to do that. I can have all the help I want. I don't think Mr. Cho lives in a rice paddy. He sounds well off. Anyone in shoes has to be well off—think how many feet there are in Hong Kong. My dear, you can count on me sending you a pair of shoes at least once a week. Isn't it wonderful?" she trilled.

Dory's mind raced. "Pix, reassure me. You didn't tell this Mr. Cho about your money and all those blue chip stocks. Tell me you didn't."

"But I did. I believe in honesty."

"Did you tell him about your drinking and smoking?"

"Bite your tongue. Do you think I want to scare him off? This is the closest thing to an offer of marriage in twenty years. I'm not a complete fool!" She emptied her glass with a loud slurp.

"What exactly is Mr. Cho going to bring into this relationship? Besides his shoes?"

Pixie's eyes glowed like marbles. "His body and his country home. I see you're skeptical. Let me put it to you another way." More scotch found its way into her glass. "God, I have a headache. I know it was that damnable Diet Pepsi. As I was saying, my dear, I'm seventy-two years old. Life is whizzing by. Just whizzing. You as well as the world must be aware of my frailties, I've made no secret of them."

Dory tried not to laugh. "I try not to think of them," she said.

"Flatulence . . . that's the worst. God, it strikes at any time and any place. I have four partials in my mouth, and that horse's rear end that tends my teeth now tells me my gums are receding. Receding! On top of that, my skin has lost its . . . its . . . zap. It just hangs. This turkey wattle under my chin is not something I try to show off to its best advantage. I have varicose veins that reappeared at the same time my tonsils tried for a comeback. My boobs are not up and out; even after the last lift they're more like down, down, down. Just yesterday I counted my hair. I have thirty-seven strands. I'm addicted to booze and cigarettes. No one loves me but you and your mother, and I think she just pretends. Now, if you were me, what would you do?"

"Go to Hong Kong."

"Right. Right, that's exactly where I'm going. I do, however, have two traits that drive men out of their minds."

"What's that?"

"I'm not discriminating and I put out!"

Dory shrieked with laughter. Dabbing at her eyes and gasping for breath, she felt better than she had in months.

Pixie stared at the young woman across the table. Something was wrong. This wasn't the Dory she knew. Not this frowzy-looking hausfrau . . . this creature clad in blue jeans and rubber boots. She glanced around the homey kitchen. Christ, the child had become domesticated. "When are you getting married?" Pixie asked bluntly. "It's not that I disapprove of living in sin, it just seems that with all this . . ." She waved her stringy arms about. ". . . that you should have something that says half is yours."

"It's a rental," Dory said soberly. "What do I need half a rental for?"

"You certainly don't look like yourself, and I can see that something is bothering you. Want to talk about it? If you do, you better replenish this bottle; I think we just killed it."

"Yes, no . . . what I mean is yes, I want to talk about it, but no, not now, but before you leave, and I don't have any more scotch. How about some wine. Neither Griff nor I are much for drinking. I didn't know we were so low. The wine is a good California chablis."

"As long as it's at least a month old I'll drink it. Remember the time we built the still on the farm? By God, I'd sell my soul for a bottle of that white lightning. *That* would certainly kill this headache."

Dory laughed. Pixie was just what she needed. The farm, as she called it, was a two-hundred-acre estate in upstate New York. The "we" she referred to was her fifth, or was it sixth, husband whom she had rescued from the clutches of the law for running shine across the line as she was driving through Tennessee in her Rolls-Royce.

"He did sing a mean ballad after a few sips of our ambrosia. God, that was an experience. Pity he had to die. When a man can't hold his liquor, he isn't much of a man. I may be dissipated, but I can hold my liquor. Mr. Cho says he's fond of rice wine. I think we'll get along very well."

"Better be careful. You know what they say about white slavers in those foreign countries. Pray Mr. Cho isn't a procurer."

"I'm praying. Now, tell me how school is going. I'm impressed, sweetie, that you decided to go for your doctorate. It's about time someone in our family did something serious. I'm sick and tired of carrying the ball for everyone. All your silly mother wants to do is play golf and get her nails done. I love her, she is my baby sister, but she doesn't know the meaning of the word fun. Don't you believe a word she tells you about our last visit," Pixie said, wagging a bony, purple tipped finger at Dory. Outrageous false eyelashes fluttered wildly as Pixie made her point.

"Let's not talk about that now. Later. With you leaving, I just want to spend time with you before Mr. Cho gobbles you up," Dory said lightly, hoping to divert Pixie from her questions.

"My life is an open book. I've told you my news." Pixie's

eyes were sharp and questioning. "What is a safe topic of conversation with you? The weather? What happened, Dory? Is this . . ." she waved her bony arms again, ". . . is this a mistake? Do you want out and can't find a way? All I have to do is look at you to know your world is upside down. What can I do? Is it money? Is it Grit, or is it you? Maybe you need to talk to your mother."

"It's Griff, not *Grit*. No, I don't need to talk to Mother. I'm working on it, Pix."

"How long is that going to take?"

"What?"

"For you to work on it? A week, a month, a year? Do you even know what it is you're working on? What is it, baby, you can tell me. We've never had secrets before. Don't close me out now." Pixie slapped her forehead so hard her wig tilted to the side. "Don't tell me you're pregnant."

"I'm not pregnant. I've been thinking about it a lot lately, though."

"Well, stop thinking right now. Parenthood is something to be taken seriously. It's not something you go into to make something else work. If things aren't working now, a baby will only compound the problem. Why don't we get comfy, slip into our lounging clothes and find something better to drink than this . . . grape water. I've had apple juice that tasted better. Do you have any vodka? How about brandy? I really don't want to open my trunk. Would you believe Mr. Cho demanded a dowry. Since he wasn't specific, I'm bringing my favorite drink that I'm sure he'll learn to love. A dowry yet, for God's sake. Did you ever hear of such a thing?"

"Sounds like a good idea. Would you like to help me decorate the house?" Dory asked, pointing to all the evergreens dripping on the kitchen floor.

"I would not. Point me to the bathroom so I can get out of these clothes."

Dory showed her the way and then headed upstairs to her bedroom to change.

Pixie felt every year of her age as she watched Dory climb

127

the stairs to the second floor. She disliked problems of any kind. How in the living hell could she go off to her fates while her beloved niece was having problems? She tried to look at it philosophically as she struggled to pull off the high, white boots. She rubbed her aching feet. She was getting old, and from the looks of things, she was also getting a few callouses on the balls of her feet. What next, she grumbled. She rummaged in her overnight bag for a Dior creation that swirled and swished when she walked. Now, if she just didn't trip and kill herself she would be all right. She wished she had remembered to ask Mr. Cho how old he was. The Oriental nature surely would prevent him from expressing comments about the ravages of time. If he refused to be a gentleman about the whole thing, she would simply pack up and leave.

She had three days to straighten out her niece. If she kept her wits about her, she might pull it off. Dory always listened to reason. She was bright, quick as a fox and razor sharp. At least she used to be. Now she appeared dull and listless. Oh, she laughed and talked, but all the sparkle, all the life, all the zest was gone from her. She had to get to the bottom of it. She also had to remember to ask what the red X's on the kitchen calendar meant.

Pixie rummaged some more in the cavernous bag and withdrew a pair of beaded Indian slipper sox. She pulled them up to her knobby knees with a flourish. She straightened her wig, patted the curls into place and then added a spritz of perfume that smelled like vanilla. She needed a drink. The headache was still with her. By God, that was the last time she was going to drink Diet Pepsi and read a magazine on a plane. Why couldn't that cheapo airline serve liquor like everyone else? She gulped down three aspirins and a sip of water. She coughed, sputtered and cursed out the Pepsi Cola Company, along with various cigarette manufacturers. Her language was ripe, colorful, and to the point. She hoped Mr. Cho would understand her penchant for choice words. If not, he had a problem. There were some things she wouldn't do for shoes.

Dory, attired in a flowing rainbow of silk, was uncorking a bottle of brandy in the living room. The fire was hissing and crackling and sending sparks up the chimney. She wished Griff were here to enjoy her Aunt Pixie. Nothing was working right. She had been looking forward to the Christmas holidays with Pixie and Griff, people she loved best in the world. Now, it would just be Griff and his mother.

Dory could feel Pixie's eyes on her, assessing her, judging her. No, Pix would never judge her. Assess her, yes, but she would never judge. She fixed a bright smile on her face and held out a three-quarters-full brandy snifter.

"The fire is nice," Pixie said, staring into the flames.

"That's one of the reasons I picked this place. Later I'll show you around the upstairs. There's a fireplace in the master bedroom. Cozy."

"I hate that word," Pixie grumbled. "Cozy is for old people who have to snuggle to keep warm or for youngsters who are necking in the back seat of a coupe. Cozy is not a word I like." She sniffed at the brandy and took a healthy swallow.

There was a hint of belligerence in Dory's tone. "I like to be cozy. I find it restful and . . . and . . ."

"Safe," Pixie said bluntly. "You're hiding behind words. I wonder if you're hiding from life, too, stuck here in this house. I want to compliment you on the bathroom. It must have taken you days."

"Weeks," Dory said grimly, not liking the turn the conversation was taking. Sometimes Pixie could get on her nerves. She didn't know everything. She didn't have all the answers. No one had all the answers.

"How's the freelance work going?" Pixie asked, watching Dory carefully.

"I haven't really started yet. I have a senator in mind. It's just a question of getting together at the right time."

"He must have been impressed when you asked him," Pixie said coolly.

"Well, actually I haven't asked him yet. I know where to

find him when I'm ready. I've been pretty busy, Pix," Dory hedged.

"I can see that. This house just screams at you. It's so goddamn . . . homey it makes me sick. If you tell me you bake bread and cookies, I'm going to throw up."

Dory flushed but didn't defend herself.

Pixie got angry as she slapped her brandy snifter down on the cocktail table. "You aren't going to school on a regular basis. Don't lie to me, Dory. You aren't doing any freelance work. You and Griff seem to be having some problems. Just what the hell is it you're doing? I don't want to hear about this homemaking nonsense. I'm not knocking homemakers. I think they're wonderful if that's what they want. What happened to your creativity? When was the last time you used your brain? When was the last time your adrenalin flowed? When was the last time you bought a new pair of shoes, a new dress? A scarf, for God's sake? I want an answer and I want it now. If it means I have to give up Mr. Cho and Hong Kong, I'm prepared to do it. There's another fool out there waiting for me somewhere. You're the most important thing in my life, Dory. You're not happy. I saw that the minute I walked through the door. When was the last time you made a concrete decision?" She hated the stricken look on Dory's face, hated the brutal tone of voice she was using.

Dory shivered and hugged her knees to her chest. "I don't know, Pix. I just don't know. Somehow I got off the track. I don't know how to get back on. Help me."

"Oh, no. This is do-it-yourself time. I'm here to listen but that's it. In the end it has to be you who makes the decisions, the choices. I can help you pick up the pieces, but don't expect more from me."

"Are you telling me it's bail-out time?"

"Only if it's right and you're comfortable with it."

"That's just it, I don't know."

"Look, Dory, we all bottom out from time to time. If we didn't fail once in a while, how would we know what it is to succeed? You have to do what's right for you. In here," Pixie said, thumping her thin chest. "There's a big world out there and you were part of it. This is another world, here in this house. If this is what you want, that's fine. If it isn't what you want, totally, then don't settle. Never settle, Dory. All your life I've told you not to settle. For if you do, you'll hate yourself in the end. We'll go into that some more later. Tell me about the friends you've made here.''

Dory told her about Sylvia and Lily. ''There were a few women I might have gotten to know better if I attended class regularly. That's it,'' Dory said defensively.

''That Lily sounds like Ms. Clean. Does she have a glass mobile too?''

In spite of herself, Dory laughed. ''Just about. She's a wonderful person, so is Sylvia. Neither of them really has anything in common with me, though. I tried, Pix, I really did. It wasn't right from the beginning. Griff admires both of them, for different reasons, of course. I was thinking about it last night. I think I tried to be both Sylvia and Lily to please him.''

Pixie yawned. Why did women always want to please men? Why did they forever put themselves second? Why? Probably because as soon as a female baby could make sounds, da da pleased the father. We're conditioned, she thought grumpily.

''How do you feel about Griff now that you've been living with him?'' Pixie asked.

''There was some adjusting to come to terms with but I did. I love him, with all my heart. What's even more wonderful, he loves me.'' It was true, he did love her. Even when he was preoccupied he would look up sometimes and smile at her. Her heart would flutter and delicious thoughts would course through her. ''I love him,'' she repeated more forcefully.

''I suppose he's a goddamn thunderbolt in the bedroom too.''

''You've got it.''

''I've heard that diminutive Orientals have . . . scaled down . . . what I mean is their . . . they aren't fully as equip . . . have you heard that?'' Pixie asked fretfully.

''It's probably some old wives' tale that started with a

131

disgruntled woman to get even with some man. Worry about it when the time comes.''

"You're probably right." Pixie's tone turned crafty. "I always found that when the New Year rolled around it was a good time to make decisions and get on the right track. New start, new everything. Diets are particularly successful because all the rich food of the holidays is gone. Expensive clothes go on sale. Bathing suits are out in full force and there's nothing to perk up a woman like a string bikini.''

"Pix, you're about as transparent as cellophane. I appreciate what you're trying to do. I know my bottom line is coming up. I'll handle it, really I will.''

"I have to believe that. You have my looks and my backbone. They've stood me in good stead for seventy-two years, and I can only hope they last as long for you. Soul searching is a precarious business. No one likes to look in the mirror and see anything less than perfection. But perfect is just a word they threw into the dictionary. It's traits like truth, justice, honesty, the American way that are important when you look in the mirror. Those things show up." Dory wouldn't have been surprised to see an invisible cape appear with Pixie tossing it over her shoulder à la Wonder Woman.

"Are you hungry?" Dory asked, wanting to change the subject.

"Yes, but I'm not going to eat. How do you think I stay so scrawny? Not by eating, that's for sure. Well, maybe something to pick on. What do you have?"

"You name it and I've probably got it. I hang out in supermarkets a lot these days.''

"Your mother told me I was as thin and flat as a swizzle stick. What do you think of that? She's jealous," she said, answering herself. "I'll eat anything as long as it doesn't have any calories.''

"That limits things a bit. How about a ham and swiss on rye with brown mustard and a piece of homemade apple pie?"

"Love it, just love it. Can I help?" This was her chance to

follow Dory into the kitchen and question her about the red X's on the calendar.

While Dory prepared the sandwiches Pixie trekked about the kitchen opening and closing cabinet doors. Neat too. She kicked at the evergreen boughs, shoving them into a corner, and peered through the glass on the back door. The cobalt sky was fast darkening. The snow had stopped, thank God. Snow was the enemy. A body could slip and fall and then they stuck pins in you to put you back together. She meandered back to the sink area. She forced a casual note into her tone. "What do the red X's mean?"

Dory stared at her aunt and then at the calendar. She'd known that sooner or later the foxy old lady was going to question her about it. Her voice was light as air when she replied, "I suppose you could say they're my bottom line."

"The big red circle, what does that mean?"

"I have to make a phone call on that day. That's the real bottom line. Here's your sandwich, Pix. I trimmed the crust off the rye since I know it's hard for you to chew."

"I knew there was a reason I put you in my will. Did I tell you I have receding gums? It's tough to grow old."

"Pixie, you'll never be old. Not to me. You want to hear something funny? Every time in my entire life that I've been in a fix you've showed up. ESP, eh?"

"Not exactly. That mother of yours is the one you can thank. She called me the other day and said she thought you could use a good dose of me ahead of schedule. Said you didn't sound like yourself. That's the main reason I'm here."

Dory's mouth dropped open. "You mean that entire business with Mr. Cho was a put-on?"

"My God, no. I was going to just call you from the airport on my way, but when your mother said you needed me, I decided that Mr. Cho would have to wait an extra three days to ravage my body. That's what they do nowadays. They ravage and plunder your body. I read that in a romance book. God, I can't wait."

Dory stared at her aunt and then burst out laughing. "Pixie, you got guts."

"So do you. Now, get on your hind legs and put them to use."

Dory cleared the table. Pixie yawned and pleaded for a nap. "I think I'll have a nightcap first," she said, picking up the brandy bottle and carrying it into the den.

"Sofa bed's all made up. Just crawl in. What time do you want me to wake you up?"

"You know I die when I fall in bed. Don't ever try to wake me. I might be having one of those lascivious dreams I love. I'll see you later."

Dory flicked on the television. The evening news was going off the air. What was she going to do with the rest of the evening? She knew from long experience that Pixie would sleep straight through till morning. The greenery. She might as well start on it. It would be nice for Pixie to see the house decorated before she left. It was a good thing she had her present. She would have plenty of time to wrap it before the older woman left. It was a gag gift, the only kind that Pixie would accept. A leather-bound journal embossed in heavy gold leaf. The perils and pitfalls in the life of Pixie Browning Balderman Simmons Caruthers Ninon Roland Fallon. The salesman had stared at her in amazement when she told him yes, I want every word on the front. It had been hard to keep a straight face. Even harder when he told her how much it was going to cost. Pixie would love it now that she was going off on another one of her escapades.

It was after midnight when Dory swept up the last pine needle. The place really did look gorgeous—festive, bright, and cheerful. That's what the holidays were all about. The huge, red velvet bows on the staircase were magnificent. The garlands of greenery were fragrant and rich. Dory drew in her breath, savoring the tangy scene. She had always loved Christmas. She looked at the six-foot evergreen in the corner. That had been a job to get into the stand but she had managed. It used to take her father, her mother, her brother and herself to stand the tree in the tub that was used for just that purpose. She had done it alone. Alone, with no help. She had surveyed the scene, calculated the best way to get the screws into the thick trunk and then done it. True, she was scratched and her robe was almost ruined, but she had done it alone. She had put up a six-foot Scotch pine Christmas tree. Tomorrow, she would string the lights and put on the decorations. It wasn't till she was climbing up the stairs that it occurred to her that she hadn't wondered once how Griff was going to react to all the decorating.

It was womb dark when she turned off the last light and settled into bed. She smiled to herself in the darkness as Pixie's loud, lusty snores wafted up the stairs.

and guess and that fuzzy sweater you're wearing
tells me you'd give a year to say what's becoming of
...
paused. "What's wrong with this, Phil?" He began

Chapter Nine

D ORY FUSSED WITH THE EVERGREEN BOUGHS OVER THE FIRE-place in the living room, adjusting a bright red bow and shiny glass ornaments. Aunt Pixie sat curled up on the sofa, watching her, from time to time complaining about the "absolutely fattening" aroma coming from the kitchen as dinner simmered in expectation of Griff's arrival home.

"How does the house look, Pix? Think Griff will approve?"

Pixie snorted in her most unladylike fashion. "Dear heart, *you* are sleeping with the man. *You* should know what he likes and doesn't like, not I. Are you always so uncertain where this young man of yours is concerned?"

Dory winced. "Ouch! Right to the point, Pix. No, I know what he likes in bed well enough. I was wondering about the decorations."

"If he exhibits the same good taste as myself, he'll think they're atrocious. Don't you think you've overdone it, Dory?" Pixie's keen eyes circled the room, taking in the extravagant and, to her mind, tacky Christmas cheer. "If you were so set upon using poinsettias, why didn't you buy real ones? Silk is overrated, don't you think?"

Dory laughed. "I suppose you're right, but the real ones need so much care. This way, I'll be able to use them again next year."

Pixie raised an eyebrow and studied her niece. "Next year? Do you mean to say you intend to make a uniform out of those faded jeans and that fuzzy sweater you're wearing? God, Dory, will it take you a year to see what's becoming of you?''

Dory bristled. "What's wrong with me? What's wrong with a woman loving her home and her man and taking the best possible care of both? Honestly, Pix, sometimes you make me feel that if I'm not wearing an Albert Nipon original I'm no one at all! I've had enough of juggling a career and a private life. I'm happy! Leave me alone, okay?''

"And Griff?" Pixie asked. Obviously the thrust of her question was lost on Dory. Pixie wanted to know if Dory thought Griff was happy with these changes in the woman he had fallen in love with.

"Griff's wonderful," Dory answered, "and you know you love him. He's a terrific man and he adores you.''

Pixie sniffed. "I'm into old smoothies myself. He isn't one of those, what do they call them, those macho types?''

"Jocks? No. He's just a great guy. Level headed. Warm and kind, loves his work. You barely met him in New York. You'll love him when you get to know him. Any guy who loves animals is okay. Animals have a sense about people.''

"How can you say that, Dory?" Pixie demanded as she drained her drink.

"Very easily. It's true. Everyone knows that animals have a keen instinct and trust only reliable, likable people.''

"Then how do you explain that Saint Bernard attacking me ten years ago when we were vacationing in Maine? I still think your mother sicced that dog on me.''

"You were carrying the brandy bottle. All that dog wanted to do was lick your face. That dog was a real love. He was mother's shadow for a good many years.''

"Yeah, until he . . . never mind, your mother is a lovely woman . . . most of the time . . . like when she isn't minding my business. She's never approved of me. She's going to kill herself with all that golf she plays. What are we going to drink when this scotch is gone?" Pixie complained as she shook the empty bottle, "cough syrup?''

Dory tried to keep a straight face. Her mother and aunt's

battles had been going on for years. "How about some vodka or gin? I have some bourbon. I think it's a hundred proof. Almost as good as your white lightning. You know something, Pix, you're *fast*." Dory grinned as Pixie trotted into the kitchen toting a bottle of bourbon.

"I hope this was a good year for bourbon," Pixie said, breaking the seal on the bottle. "I never really got into bourbon. But when in Rome . . ."

"I could have Griff stop and pick up some more scotch on his way home."

"What? And have him think I'm a drunk? Never. I'll suffer with this bourbon." Dory watched in awe as Pixie filled her wine glass almost to the brim.

"He'd never think that, Pix. And if he did, he's too much of a gentleman to say so."

"What kind of wine are you serving with dinner? And what is that mess you keep stirring?"

"Red. And this is stew. Very nourishing, lots of vitamins. Crusty French bread and a cherry pie. I baked the pie last month and put it in the freezer."

"I can't eat all that," Pixie said in horror. "What time will Griff be here?"

"Any minute now. Move over so I can set the table."

"You mean you don't use paper plates? Who's going to wash all these dishes?"

"The dishwasher. Don't worry, I remember that soapy water makes brown spots on your hands. I wouldn't dream of asking you to do dishes."

"You're such a wonderful child," Pixie said, tilting the bourbon bottle.

Griff arrived minutes later. Dory stood by and watched while Pixie and Griff gave each other a big hug.

"What are you drinking?" Griff asked. "Looks good. How about making a tired man a scotch and water?"

"She can't. There isn't any more," Pixie said, sipping at her drink.

"Oh, I thought we had a full bottle. That's okay, how about some brandy?"

"There isn't any," Pixie said.

Griff nodded. "What you're saying is you drank the scotch and the brandy, and if I want a drink, I better take some of this bourbon or that's going to be gone too."

"You got it. And when that's gone it's cough syrup for the both of us. I do like a fully stocked liquor cabinet," Pixie complained.

"I thought I had one." Griff grinned at Dory.

"That's right, you did, but you had nothing in reserve. That's the key word, reserve."

"I'll remember that. Where are you going with all those suitcases? Looks like the Grand Tour."

"I'm going to Hong Kong to get married."

Griff choked and sputtered. Dory wasn't sure if it was Pixie's declaration or that he had just happened to notice her fringed Indian slippers.

"Who . . . who's the lucky man?"

"Probably a gentleman of dubious nature. I haven't met him yet. Don't look so shocked. We've been pen pals for a while. He writes a mean letter, or at least that's what the man at the Chinese embassy tells me. He translates them for me since they're written in Chinese."

Dory filled a bowl with stew and set it in the middle of the table. A long loaf of crusty bread and a small crock of butter, along with a plate of fresh cut vegetables, were set on a mat near Pixie.

"I'll just pick," she said, filling her plate to the edge. "This girl is a whiz, a pure whiz. I had no idea you could cook like this, Dory. You must be very proud of her, young man."

Pixie made a pretense of sipping at her drink while she watched Griff's face. His eyes were blank and his face actually stilled. It was the first time she had ever seen that happen. A writer says such things in a novel, and the reader tries to imagine what a face looks like when it stills. Now Pixie was actually seeing it happen. Nothing moved on Griff's face. Then he smiled, but the blank look remained in his eyes. "Very proud. Wait till you taste the cherry pie."

"I have no intention of tasting the cherry pie. It's obscene

139

to serve pie after a big meal like this," Pixie said as she ripped off a chunk of bread. "I can only eat the center or one of my four partials will come unglued."

"That makes sense," Griff said.

"I'll donate an emergency room to your clinic if you can use one. Do animals have emergency rooms? I want my name over the door. Is that okay with you?"

Griff swallowed hard, his eyes imploringly on Dory. Was the old lady so plastered she didn't know what she was saying or did she mean it? Dory kept on eating, refusing to meet his gaze. "I . . . I think that can be arranged. Our clinic is new and we could certainly use another room. Are you sure you want to do this? What I mean is, you don't have to feel you . . ." he floundered for words.

"What you're trying to say in a tactful manner, young man, is you think I'm blitzed and tomorrow I won't remember. Ha! I can hold my liquor and I get my liver checked once a month at the same time I go to the proctologist. At my age you can't leave anything to chance. When I told the doctor about these headaches he told me to stop reading. Eyestrain. So simple and I was so worried. This wine is terrible, Dory. Of course I'll remember. I love animals. Animals have a sense about people . . . don't they, Dory?"

"Have some more bourbon," Griff offered. Dory continued to stare at her plate.

"With stew? Goodness, a body could get sick doing something like that. Maybe with my coffee." Pixie leaned back in her chair and lit a cigarette. "Are you sure now that my name will be over the door of the emergency room? And the word 'Emergency' clearly painted on the door. That's a must. I love to do good deeds as long as everyone knows I do them. I never hide my light in a closet."

"That's under a bushel, Pix," Dory said.

"Whatever. I'll call a banker in the morning before I leave. Send me a picture. A colored one, and then another one when the first patient is treated."

"I'll do that," Griff gasped.

"I told you, Dory, I couldn't eat any of that pie. My God,

there must be at least a thousand calories in one piece. Nuts and raisins, too. A small piece, I'll just pick.''

When Dory carried the last dish to the dishwasher Pixie got up from the table. "I fear one of those damnable headaches is coming on. Dory, you should have stopped me from reading the *National Enquirer*."

Griff was full of concern for Dory's aunt. "I have some strong headache pills. Can I get you a couple? I know what it is to get a headache."

"Good heavens, no. Medicine of any kind never touches this body," Pixie said. "I'll just take this bourbon with me in case I need something to make me sleep. You can always count on a good bourbon to put you to sleep. Dory, it was a wonderful dinner; even though I just picked I could tell. Don't get up, dear boy, these feet can still find the way." With a wild flourish she picked up the bourbon bottle and succeeded in knocking the crust off the cherry pie. She grabbed a piece of the crust to "nibble" on and made her way to her room.

Griff cleared his throat. "Tell me she's real. The truth now."

In spite of herself Dory laughed. "She's about as real as they come. She grows on you is what she does."

"Are you telling me she's serious about the emergency room?"

"She takes her 'good deeds' as seriously as she does her drinking. If I were you, though, I'd make sure her name is very big. Very big. It wouldn't hurt to make sure it gets in the papers. She's big on papers too. Especially the *National Enquirer*. She reads it from cover to cover."

"What say you and I have a drink in front of the fire? I have to unwind after that lady. She's a piece of work, your aunt. Or did she drink all the good stuff? What do you two have planned?"

Dory giggled. "Every last drop. I can make us some hot chocolate. There's some hot coffee left. We're just going to wing it. Visit. Talk. Old times, that kind of thing. Why do you ask?"

Griff rummaged in his pocket and withdrew a thin envelope. "Here, I finally remembered to pick up the theatre tickets you wanted. Why don't you and Pixie go. You won't miss me. The two of you will have a ball."

Dory's entire body froze. How cool he was being. How blasé. He didn't want to go to the theatre with her. Not any more. Before he would have gone simply to please her and pretend he was enjoying himself. Was it too much effort to pretend these days? And that look of relief on his face when he held out the tickets to her. Maybe she was being unfair. Maybe Griff was simply being generous in giving up the tickets so Pixie could enjoy herself. Don't think about it now, her inner voice warned.

"What's it going to be, hot chocolate or coffee?" she asked brightly.

"It's not a drink I want, it's you. Come on, woman, let's you and me snuggle up in front of the fire and make wild, passionate love."

Dory linked her arm in Griff's. "Best offer I've had all day. I'm going to hold you to that wild part."

Griff smiled lecherously. "You're on."

"But not in front of the fire. Pix might hear us. Up in our room, okay?"

"Okay." Griff's voice was husky and sexy and his arms were warm and so strong.

Dory's eyes went to the unfinished dishes. "Give me a minute and I'll be right up." She pushed him toward the doorway. "Two minutes," she called after him, rushing back to the sink to rinse out the coffee cups and put the milk and pie in the fridge. One chore led to another and it was nearly twenty minutes before she climbed the stairs to their room and the softly glowing fire Griff had lit. He was sprawled on their bed, head cradled in his arms, fast asleep.

There was a sadness in Pixie's eyes when she said her good-bys at the airport. She clutched her Christmas gift tightly in mittened hands. "Pix, you're the only woman in the world who would wear mittens with a sable coat. I hope your first entry in the journal proves to be memorable,'' Dory whispered as she hugged the old lady, careful not to disturb the freshly curled wig. "Write. Send it to Mom's house and she'll see that I get it."

"Gotcha." Pixie kissed Griff soundly and waved airily to Dory as she bounded up the ramp behind a group of chattering youngsters.

Entering the town house the couple was assaulted with the scent of fresh evergreens. "I love it, reminds me of when I was a kid. I still can't believe you put that tree up yourself. You are absolutely amazing," Griff said, kissing her softly on the neck. "Hmmmmn, you do wild, wonderful things to me. Let's forget dinner and go to bed. We haven't been spending enough time together and it's all my fault. I didn't realize we were going to be so damn busy. Usually, when you open a clinic like ours it takes a good year to become established. I guess John's and Rick's fame has spread. I was the one who got that colt to nurse, though. There was a congenital obstruction in the pharynx which required emergency surgery. Almost lost the little beauty. It was touch and go for a few hours."

"That's wonderful, Griff."

"Nothing like success to make you feel on top of the world. I could slay dragons right now or make love to the most beautiful girl in the world. I think I like girls better than slaying dragons."

"I should hope so. What say we shower together? You soap me, I soap you." Dory grinned devilishly.

"Now I know that's the best offer I've had in over a week."

"Has it been a week?"

"It has, but that's only if you're counting." It was a week. A week today, as a matter of fact. Dory couldn't be so caught up in her own world that she didn't know or care how long it had been. The thought bothered him and took the edge off his excitement. Dory's sexual appetites were as healthy and lusty as his own.

Their lovemaking was animal-like in its intensity. As he

drifted off to sleep Griff felt vaguely cheated somehow. Dory lay wide awake. Why was it sex put men to sleep and awakened women? She lay quietly trying to decipher how she felt. Certainly not unloved. Griff had said the right words, done the right things, so why did she have to "figure out" how she felt? She should *know*. She should be feeling something, some afterglow, some invisible high that all lovers felt, that she used to feel. Instead, she felt . . . her mind sought for the right word . . . impatient.

Dory's last conscious thought before drifting off to sleep was that she envied Pixie and her free spirit ways.

Griff roused Dory when he finished showering. "Don't you have an early morning class today?"

"Hmmmmmm," Dory replied.

"Up and at 'em, tiger, let's go." Griff jabbed at her playfully. "We all have to work. Remember that old adage, 'He who does not contribute does not eat.' "

All semblance of sleep was gone. While his voice might sound playful, Dory caught the nuance that said it just wasn't so. "All right," she said, swinging her legs over the side of the bed. Her next thought came out of nowhere. "Griff, I'm going to take the shuttle into New York. There's one that leaves around twelve or so. I'll try to make it back tonight, but if I get held up, I'll return first thing in the morning." It was on the tip of her tongue to say she hoped he didn't mind. Instead, she left it as the statement of fact she intended.

Griff paused in the act of tying his dark tie. "Great," he said. "Have a ball and I think you should stay overnight. Don't worry about me, I can get something to eat from Ollie's Trolley on the way home."

Dory refused to think about Griff's exuberance as she showered. She would not think about it. No way was she going to touch that one.

D-Day. Red X day. Time to keep her word and get in touch with Lizzie. Time to speak to Katy. Time for a trip to *Soiree*. Time to drag David Harlow out of the dark recesses of her mind.

Two weeks till New Year's. Two weeks and one day. The

new year, a time to cast the old aside and bring in the new. Decision time.

An hour later the king-size bed resembled a harem in disarray. Clothes and shoes were everywhere. Dejectedly, Dory sat on the edge of the bed. Nothing fit. At that moment she would have sold her body for a skirt with an elastic waist. If she started playing with moving buttons or half pulling zippers she would throw the line of the garment off. And her hair, God, what a mess. Freshly shampooed would do nothing for the old luster. How long had it been since she patronized a beauty shop and had a rinse, just for highlights? Ages. Lily's home barber shop could hardly be called a salon. She was a mess. Lord, even some of her shoes were tight across the instep. That was from running around in scruffy sneakers all day.

Eyeing the confusion all around her, Dory felt angry . . . and impatient. Angry that she had allowed things to get to this point and impatient to be on her way to the city.

A curling iron might help. Her fox coat, if she kept it on, would certainly camouflage her weight gain. Makeup would be no problem. She did look a little puffy around the eyes, but by the time she was ready to leave the swelling would be gone.

Pixie should be halfway to Hong Kong by now. The thought made Dory smile. Go for it, Pix, because if you don't, there ain't no one out there gonna do it for you.

Dory had enjoyed the long talks she'd had with Pixie during her three-day visit. Not once had Pixie even attempted to tell her what to do. She listened and then prattled on about her own adventures and misadventures. Always her piercing gaze would lock with Dory's to be sure she was getting her subtle messages.

It was another hour before Dory returned all the clothes to their scented hangers and piled the shoes back in their marked boxes. She made the bed and straightened the bathroom. Makeup was applied swiftly and deftly; the curling iron whizzed through her hair to create a slight curl which she misted with hairspray. She wasn't exactly like the old Dory but she could pass a quick muster.

Dory checked her purse for her checkbook, her wallet, and an ample supply of tissues. She wouldn't take an overnight bag. If she decided to stay in New York she would take a quick run to Saks and pick up a few things. The Christmas-gift check from Pixie, which was almost sufficient for a down payment on a house, was folded carefully. Citibank would applaud her when she deposited the check. Pixie's brand of security.

The thermostat was adjusted, all the lights off, the garage door open, the car warming up, the coffee pot unplugged. She felt an unexpected exhilaration as she closed the door behind her. Mechanically, she tried the knob to be certain it was locked.

Dory drove to the airport and parked the car, pocketed the parking stub and walked to the entrance. Standing in line at the ticket counter, she impatiently watched the round clock high on the wall tick off the minutes. If things didn't speed up, she would miss the flight that was due to take off for New York in less than twenty minutes.

As the ticket agent completed arrangements with a traveler and the line moved forward, Dory suddenly became aware of someone watching her. Turning to her left, she focused on a tall, well-dressed gentleman, who was brazenly focusing on her. Dory felt a surge of sudden confidence. She knew the soft grays and silvers of the natural fox coat did wonders for her pale blonde hair, and the bright raspberry silk blouse with its complementary wool tweed skirt offset the pink of her cheeks. Although her black Etienne Aigner boots were still feeling tight across the instep, they were the finishing touch to her outfit.

The man, dressed in a dark brown suit, with a luxurious overcoat of brushed suede, continued to stare approvingly in Dory's direction. It felt good to be admired and she warmed to a flush in spite of herself. She knew she would only have to give him a glance of encouragement and he would approach her. Not in the habit of picking up men in airports, Dory forced herself to look away. Was she so desperate for approval that she would resort to flirting with total strangers? Still, there was something about this man she recognized; she had seen him somewhere before; she knew she had. Where? Through the advertising department at *Soiree*? At Lincoln Center? Skating in Rockefeller Center? A touch on her arm.

"Excuse me," a deep masculine voice was saying, "I believe you dropped this." He held up one of her slim leather gloves.

Searching through her pockets, Dory realized he was correct. "Thank you. I'm always losing gloves. I suppose I should pin them to my sleeves the way mother did when I was a little girl." Looking into his startlingly clear blue eyes, Dory felt her smile deepen. She realized with a certain alarm that this stranger was still holding the hand into which he had pressed her glove. He was tall, good looking, and his obvious interest in her was flattering.

"By any chance do you have a few minutes for a cup of coffee? I feel as though I've been struck by Kismet." The blue eyes captured hers, making her heart race with excitement. There was a certain confidence about this man, as though he could instantly recognize what he wanted and could unerringly set his course for it. The words "charisma" and "power" kept bouncing through Dory's brain.

"I would like that," she told him honestly, "however, my plane leaves in a very few minutes. I'm going to New York." Now why had she told him that?

His disappointment was obvious. "Perhaps when you return to the capital then?" he asked, reaching into his inside jacket pocket to give her his card. "Please, call me. I've only just found you and you're flying away."

The ticket agent interrupted, "Can I help you? Miss? Did you wish to purchase a ticket?"

Flustered, Dory stepped up to the counter. "I'm sorry . . . I mean . . . I must go."

"You have my card, call, won't you?" A small salute and he was gone.

The ticket agent smiled warmly, noticing the situation between Dory and the handsome man who was now walking out of the terminal. In purchasing her ticket and rummaging through her purse for her American Express card, Dory never noticed that the business card he had given her had fallen to the floor.

On the forty-five-minute flight to New York Dory thought about her encounter with the stranger. It felt good to be admired. Just a bit of harmless flirting, she told herself, feeling slightly guilty about Griff, knowing that if she'd had the time she would have joined the stranger for coffee. Harmless flirting, she told herself. It was silly to keep thinking of the man as a stranger; he'd given her his card and his name would be on it. Suddenly, very, very curious about who he was and what he did for a living, she searched the pocket of her coat for his business card. It was gone. Lost. She had lost it, and some niggling fear told her she was losing her grip on more than just a card handed her by a stranger.

Chapter Ten

IN THE *SOIREE* OFFICES KATY WELCOMED DORY WITH OPEN ARMS
while the girls in the outer office hovered around, waiting for
her to recognize them. She called each by name, pecked some
on the cheek, smiled at others as she shook hands. God, it felt
wonderful.

"Anyone water my plants? I'm into plants now." She
grinned to a laughing Katy.

"Just like a jungle. When you move down the hall I'll be
sure they follow you," Katy teased.

When. Not if. When she returned to *Soiree* was what Katy
meant.

Dory felt smug as she accepted a cup of coffee from one of
the secretaries. She smiled and thanked her. "What's new?"

"Not a whole hell of a lot. I was going to call you at least
a thousand times but Lizzie forbade it. She said she made a
bargain with you and that included no phone calls, except for
emergencies. I managed. Not well, but I managed." Katy
shrugged. "Your replacement . . . she isn't you. I want to
transfer to your new offices with you. Can you swing it?"

The smug feeling stayed with Dory as she sipped the
coffee. Hell yes, she could swing it. She would be the boss.
If she decided to return, that is. Her visit seemed to convince
everyone that that was her intention. Maybe she had been too
hasty. She could have just picked up the phone instead of

149

making the trip in person. She didn't want to rain on Katy's parade.

Was there such a thing as a creative high? A high brought on by friends and fellow workers. A business . . . a job . . . when had she last felt like this? So long ago she forgot what the feeling was like.

"How about some pastry?"

"No thanks. I'm dieting. Look and weep." Dory laughed as she opened the fox coat.

"My God," Katy said.

"That's what I said when I read the scale. Salads from now on, that's it. It really sneaked up on me."

"Is Lizzie expecting you?"

"Not in person. A phone call, perhaps. She's here, isn't she? What's new with the adoption?"

"She's here. As a matter of fact she's been coming in at seven every morning to get caught up before she leaves. The baby arrives January first."

Dory's heart started to pound. She could feel the beginnings of an anxiety attack. God, not here, not in front of Katy, she pleaded silently. Relax, get hold of yourself. It's your choice, your decision. Nothing has to be decided today. "But I thought . . ." Damn, why did she sound like she was whimpering?

"We all thought it would be another three months. What can I tell you? The mother delivered prematurely. The baby was in an incubator for a while. She may even get it for Christmas. We're all hoping. It's a girl, just what she wanted!"

A vision of her decorated town house flashed before Dory's eyes. Her first Christmas with Griff. Dinner with his mother. Lily and Rick would stop by. Sylvia would have them over for breakfast or brunch, depending on the condition of her house. Presents. Mistletoe and holly. Carols and church.

"Dory, this shouldn't mess up your doctorate. Remember, I checked it out . . . you can continue your studies at night at Columbia. It'll delay things a bit, but you're so set on achieving your doctorate, a few more months shouldn't make all that much difference. How's it going, anyway?" Katy asked cheerfully, as though it were a foregone conclusion that anything Dory tackled was soon accomplished.

"Oh, fine, fine!" Dory lied, feeling the old guilt about how she had let herself down.

Dory set her empty cup on Katy's desk. "I'll trundle along now and visit with Lizzie. I want to make the bank and do some shopping. I think I'll stay over at the Hyatt. Could you book me a room? If you're free, we could have dinner together. My treat. We have so much catching up to do. Do you think your husband will mind?"

"Mind? He'll be delighted. Tonight is his bowling night anyway. I'll stay late and catch up on some of my own work. Meet you in the lobby at seven. Is that okay with you?"

"Fine." Dory hugged her friend and waved to her co-workers. She was stifling in the fox coat, but she refused to take it off. If she was stupid enough to gain so much weight, then she would suffer for it. Wearing the heavy fur in the office was punishment enough.

Lizzie greeted her warmly, her shrewd eyes assessing Dory. "I would have settled for a call," she said softly.

"You look positively radiant, Lizzie. Katy told me the news. I'm so happy for you."

"I feel radiant. Hell, I am radiant, you're right. I don't think I've ever been so happy. Sit down, let's talk."

Dory let the fox slip from her shoulders. She waited for Lizzie to take the initiative.

"As I said, I would have settled for a phone call. But, don't misunderstand, I'm glad you came. Wanted a look-see, huh? Did you miss it?"

"Yes, I did miss it. Yes, I wanted a look-see, as you put it. And yes, I put on some weight. I'm dieting now. Nothing fits." Lizzie said nothing, her gaze sharp and pointed as she assessed Dory.

"I'm going to need an answer by Monday, Dory. I wish I could give you longer but I can't. I hope you understand."

"I do. I'll call you Monday morning," Dory said quietly. If there was ever a time for an anxiety attack, this was it,

Dory thought. She waited. Nothing happened. She grinned at Lizzie.

Lizzie grinned back. "Bought any nice shoes lately?"

"I'm on my way to Saks right now."

"Dory, whatever you decide, it's all right with me. I want us to remain friends. I know you'll do what's right for you."

"Count on it. Make sure you send pictures of the baby."

"Count on it." Lizzie laughed.

"I'll talk to you on Monday."

Dory's first stop was Citibank. She cashed an astronomical check, deposited Pixie's check, and started out for Saks. She treated herself to a haircut, a manicure, and pedicure. Her next stop was the shoe department, where she bought four pairs of shoes and two pairs of boots. At the last minute she picked up a pair of naughty, feathery slippers. I don't need them but I want them. That's reason enough, she told herself as she got into the elevator.

Dory shopped till the store closed. She waited patiently for the doorman to get her a taxi. She could have walked; everyone in New York walked. But this was a day to pamper herself. A taxi ride was no big deal. She was all grown up now and could make her own decisions. About time, she thought.

Dinner with Katy was a pleasure. They sat for hours over wine spritzers and salad. They talked about everything and nothing but mostly about Katy's work and Lizzie's new baby. Eating was a time for relaxing, Katy said, and they could get down to the nitty gritty when they got back to Dory's room at the Hyatt.

It was after ten when both women kicked off their shoes in the hotel suite. Dory ordered espresso and Amaretto from room service. It arrived within minutes. Dory added a generous tip to the waiter. Settled comfortably in the armchair, she faced Katy. "You're dying to know, I can tell. I don't know where to start. Everything is so mixed up. I'm so confused, I don't know which way to turn any more."

Katy's friendly face showed concern for her friend. "A relationship is no different than a marriage. You have to work at it. Both of you. As far as I can see the only difference is that you can walk out without going to a lawyer.''

Dory sipped at her drink. ''It's not one of those he did this, he didn't do that, I did it all, things. It wasn't anything like that. I really think it's me, not Griff. I got off the track. My God, it got to the point where I was having anxiety attacks and I wasn't me any more. I even went so far as to think I should have a baby. Thank God I had enough sense to know that was a mistake. A baby would only compound the problem.''

''At least you're thinking clearly.''

''Now, yes. And even now I'm not sure. I could have called Lizzie today the way I said I would, but at the eleventh hour I decided to come in. I needed to come here today. I haven't really made a decision. I have to talk to Griff.''

''That's understandable. Did you tell all this to Lizzie?''

''Tell Lizzie! You must be joking. Lizzie read me like a book. She gave me till Monday and said I have to give her a concrete decision. She's being more than fair; she'll have her decision. Hey, Katy, this is my life we're talking about.''

''Tell me about it, oh wise and wonderful friend.''

''Don't you have anything to say, some advice to offer?''

''No way. I never stick my nose in other people's business even if they are my best friend. I want us to keep what we have. What I will say to you is get your priorities in order and work from there.''

''I'm trying.''

''Not good enough. You have to do it. Trying is for beginners. Jump in with both feet and do it,'' Katy said, swallowing the bitter coffee.

''I could screw up and regret it later.''

''That's a chance we all take every day when we climb out of bed. You'll live with it because you have to. It's simple. You're going to do what you have to do because it's best for you. Can't you see that, Dory?''

How patient she was, this loyal friend. ''It's easier to cop out and blame other people and other things.''

Katy laughed. ''I know all about that. I've been down

some rocky roads and I weathered it. You will too. You're what we used to call 'good people' where I came from. Hey, have you bought any new shoes lately? What's the count?''

"Today I bought four pairs and two pairs of boots. I didn't buy any while I was in Virginia. I lived in sneakers. I'm going to burn them tomorrow when I get back. I detest sneakers. I hate them with a passion.''

Katy had never seen such a wild look on Dory's face or heard so much vehemence in her voice.

"Hey, if sneakers aren't your thing, that's okay. Don't get hyper.''

"See, see what I mean. It's coming out now. At home I held it in and was . . . I was . . . damn it, I was pleasant.''

"There's nothing wrong with being pleasant.''

"Oh, yes there is. Especially if you feel like yelling or voicing your opinion. Anger is a healthy emotion. Did you know that, Katy?''

"I should. I give vent to it at least a hundred times a day both here and home.''

"I never did that in all the time I've been living with Griff. I was . . . I was just damn pleasant. I didn't want him upset. I wanted to make things perfect for him. I waited on him hand and foot. I made gourmet meals. I decorated that damn town house till I was blue in the face. I made it a place for him to be proud of. I put him first. I copped out on school. I copped out on myself, on everything.''

"Is that what he wanted?'' Katy asked softly.

Dory stared at Katy for long minutes. "I don't know. He accepted everything. He never argued or lost his temper with me. I made myself over for him. I did everything I could to make it work.''

"But is that what he *wanted?*'' Katy persisted.

"I don't know. I honestly don't know.''

"Oh, yes you do. You know all right or you wouldn't be sitting here right now. It's easier to pick up the phone. But you made the trip. You left here a successful career woman. A woman who had her own apartment, was confident, had her own portfolio. How many times did I hear you talk about your small investments that you broke your back for? Every girl in that office would have sliced off her right arm for half of what you exuded. Just half. *That* was the woman Griff fell in love with and wanted to marry. Am I right or not?''

"Okay, okay. I think you're right. Love is love. Inside I tried to be the same person I was back here in New York. Just because I kept house shouldn't mean that I . . . oh, Katy, I screwed up. I know what happened. I tried to be all things. That person back in the town house wasn't me. It never was, even from the first day. I'm no Susy Homemaker. I'm me. Sylvia and Lily irritated the hell out of me. I put on a good front but I could feel myself churning every time I had to be in their company. God, I tried. I really tried. The more I tried the unhappier I was. You're right. I turned into a caricature of myself. There were times when I would catch Griff looking at me as if I had sprouted a second head. I couldn't understand it. I thought it was what he wanted. I did everything to please him.''

"You did everything but be yourself, the Dory he fell in love with. If he wanted a homemaker he could have hired a maid. He wanted you. The real you. The you that's sitting here now talking to me.''

"The whole thing is a little hard to swallow. I wasn't fair to Griff or myself. I cheated both of us.''

"There must have been some good times, especially in the beginning,'' Katy said gently. She hated the tormented look in her friend's eyes. Better for her to see it, and help, than for Dory to go on and on and never make a decision. It was too easy to sink in, to say the hell with it. She should know, she had gone through the same thing a long time ago.

"Of course there were good times, wonderful times. I could never forget them. Never. But they're memories now, Katy. I sound bitter, I guess, but I want you to know I wouldn't change anything for all the money in the world. I needed that time with Griff and I think he did too. We'll both be better for it. It just didn't work. If I hadn't packed up and gone I would always have regretted it. Like Pixie says, Go for it, if it isn't right you'll know soon enough. That lady never steered me wrong yet. From here on in I have to do what's best for me. I have to get my life back. It's not going to be easy. I love Griff. Maybe I'll always love him. But I love other things too. I love New York, I love this job here at the magazine. I love that jungle out there, I love life. Maybe I do want it all. There's nothing wrong with that. I don't have to compromise, I don't have to give up things, I don't have to turn myself inside out to get it all. All I have to do is get my priorities straight. Right or wrong?''

"Sounds familiar, Dory. Familiar and accurate. You're on the right track. See what talking to an old friend can do for you?'' Katy hugged her friend tightly.

"Thanks, Katy. You really helped me.''

"Hey, you did it yourself. I just listened. Did I give you even one piece of advice? Did I say you were right or wrong?''

"You're right! God, I really did it all myself, didn't I? I figured it out. I've got it together. Well, almost. I have a few more hurdles but I can handle them. I might even have a setback but I know where I'm going. And before you leave I have to know how the profile and layout with Pixie came out.''

Katy laughed. "It's going to be one of the best pieces *Soiree* ever put out, I can tell you that. The feedback we've been getting is fantastic. Pixie was so divine to work with. She asked about doing a follow-up next year—said she'd come all the way from Hong Kong—and she keeps questioning us about talk-shows. Talk-shows yet!''

"I'm glad Lizzie decided to go with it. Was it hard to get around what Pixie calls 'old age horny'?''

"Good lord, no. It's a work of art. Exquisite taste, I can tell you that. That article generated so much interest, the entire board came to see the last shooting session. They loved Pixie, particularly after that bash at the Sign of the Dove. I sent you the last in-house release, didn't you read it? Harlow gave you full credit, two whole paragraphs as a matter of fact. He said, and this is a direct quote, 'We have Dory Faraday to thank for her insight and her courage in bringing this matter to our attention. It's a topic that most magazines would shy away from. Always being a front runner, *Soiree* and the board feel that Faraday showed remarkable foresight in laying the groundwork for such a remarkable profile.' And he went on and on, giving you fragrant bouquets. I mailed it to you days ago.''

''Not a word yet. I'll probably find it waiting when I get home tomorrow. When does it come out?''

''Spring issue.''

''Send a dozen copies to Aunt Pixie in Hong Kong.''

''What is she really doing over there?'' Katy asked.

''She's doing her thing. She stopped by for three days before she left. She hasn't changed a bit. She'll live to be a hundred and enjoy every day of it. Griff loves her; they get along wonderfully.''

''How could he not like her? She's one of the most remarkable women I ever met. Age certainly does have its moments. Give her my regards when you write to her.''

''I'll do that. It was great talking with you, Katy. I missed you. I've missed all of this. I'll be in touch.''

Katy wrapped her arms around Dory. ''Any time. See you.''

Dory drew the deadbolt and changed for bed. She'd think about all this tomorrow when she got back to Virginia.

Dory deplaned the following morning at National Airport. It was close to the lunch hour and the winter sun was glinting brightly through the long glass windows in the terminal. As she waited for the conveyor to deliver up her packaged shoe boxes her eyes kept swinging over the travelers. It was silly to think she might see the man she'd met the afternoon before, but she couldn't help herself.

Feeling more disloyal to Griff than she liked, she scooped her parcels off the conveyor and headed for the parking lot.

The town house seemed alien with its wealth of greenery. For some reason it irritated her. She adjusted the thermostat and hung up her fox coat. Annoyance cloaked her when she looked at the messy bed. She hadn't missed the littered breakfast table with the toast crumbs and empty coffee cup. Woman's work! she thought nastily. One leg of Griff's pajamas hung over the hamper. A wet and soggy towel was wadded up in the basin. One slipper was stuck under the door, preventing it from closing. "The hell with it!" Dory exploded as she made her way downstairs. She fixed a cup of strong, black coffee and sat down to drink it. When she was finished she would exercise for an hour and start to get back into shape. A salad for lunch and dinner and she would be off to a good start. Griff could have steak and salad. No more gourmet meals. No more a lot of things.

Four days to make a decision. Her eyes flew to the calendar. Four days. Ninety-six hours. Five thousand seven hundred and sixty minutes.

Griff. She had to think about Griff. If she went back, what would happen to their relationship? It was a known fact that distance did nothing for love. It did not make the heart grow fonder. Could she make it without Griff? Did she really want to go back? When she had left the *Soirée* offices she had stood outside, looking up at the office windows. She recalled saying, "This is where it's at." The words stunned her at the time and gave her food for thought as she made her way uptown to Saks.

If that was true, what about her time here with Griff? What did that count for? Was it a trial, a jumping-off point? Exactly what was it? A haven. A safe place to be for a while. Not permanently, but for a while.

When had "not permanently" become a part of her thinking? When she made the decision to take a leave of absence and return to school and move in with Griff, some secret part of her believed it was forever. It was to be a modern relationship that would eventually lead to marriage. She could admit that to herself now.

She loved Griff. Loved him heart and soul. A part of her would die if she left; this she knew as sure as she knew she needed to breathe to stay alive. But she needed more. There was no challenge here. She was making so little contribution to life. Her stomach churned with her thoughts. God, what should she do? How had she ever allowed herself to get to this point? Finding no answers, her eyes swept to the calendar and the red X's.

She was across the room to the phone in a lightning quick moment. She flipped the calendar to the back "note" page and punched out the number she wanted. Her breathing quickened as she waited for someone on the other end of the phone to pick it up. "Senator Carlin's office. May I help you?"

"Yes. This is Dory Faraday. Several months ago *Soiree* magazine spoke to both you and the senator about doing a profile of him when the Senate offices adjourned for the holidays. I'd like to discuss a mutual date if he's in."

"As a matter of fact you just caught him. He's already packed to leave to return to New York for the holidays. One moment, I'll fetch him. He's talking to someone in the outer office."

An omen. It was an omen, she was sure of it. Dory's throat tightened as she waited for Drake Collins to come on the line. Even though she couldn't be seen, she brushed her hair back from her forehead and rubbed her index finger across her lips.

"Miss Faraday. *Soiree* magazine said you'd be getting in touch with me. I thought you'd forgotten." His voice was deep. A smile was in that voice, she could hear it.

"Senator, that's very amusing. I don't think the woman has been born who could forget you. If I'm to believe your press, you have charisma. That's the main reason I want to do this profile. You could consider it a public thank-you for all those breathless females who ran to the voting booth."

A low chuckle came over the wire, sending a chill up Dory's arms. "My first rule when taking office was never to get caught up in my own press releases."

Dory laughed. "When can we get together?"

"I'm free from the day after Christmas until the third of January when we go back in session. I believe my secretary gave you my home address."

"Yes, she did. I want to interview you on your home turf and perhaps do some pictures of you both there and in

159

Washington. And at Ollie's Trolley, complete with pictures of you and Nick. That's a must."

"Will it be a problem for you to come to New York?" Was that an anxious tone in his voice? Dory wasn't sure, but if it was, she liked the idea.

"No," she replied without hesitation. "Tell me, is there a particular lady in your life?" She held her breath, waiting for a reply. "Senator, I'm not asking for myself. If there is someone close to you, our readers would like to know. Pictures of the two of you together having lunch, jogging in Central Park, that sort of thing."

The low chuckle came over the wire again, but no answer to her question was forthcoming. Dory licked at her lips and smiled. "You're engaged and married to your career, is that it?"

"Now, you're talking my language. Until the right lady comes along we'll go with that. I'd like to chat with you longer, but I want to catch the shuttle. I'll tell you what. Let me get settled in, pick up a few groceries and I'll call you back tomorrow and we can set up a date. Have a nice Christmas, Miss Faraday."

"I will, Senator, and . . . enjoy your holidays."

Dory stared at the phone for long minutes after she replaced the receiver. It was a new beginning. Her first major decision since moving into the town house. It was something concrete, something she could get her teeth into. Something she wanted to do, damn it. Something she was going to like doing.

Picking up the phone once again, Dory punched out the number for *Soiree*, catching Katy just before she left for lunch. "Katy, I've made contact with Senator Collins and now I'm in a fix. Can you wire me everything we have on him? If I'm going to appear intelligent on this interview, I've got to know something about the man. Express mail would get it here before noon tomorrow and that'll give me a chance to read it over."

Dory felt good. She'd gotten the ball rolling, and all she

had to do was follow along. It was easy! Why had it seemed so difficult during these past months?

The niggling voice Dory lived with questioned her about Georgetown. *An excuse for me to move here with Griff without the commitment of marriage*, she answered it honestly. *I'm not ready for that doctorate, not yet. Maybe never. Maybe next year, but it will be for the right reasons. I have things to do, places to go. I'm just not ready.*

She certainly was clearing all the cobwebs out of her mental closets today.

How she hated that kitchen calendar. The notation in green lettering told her Griff's mother would arrive the following day.

Esther Michaels was a lovely woman, a young, fiftyish widow running a small advertising agency and making a go of it. She and Dory had gotten along well at their initial meeting, engineered by Griff, in New York. The talk over dinner had centered on the theater. Esther was into theater, the ballet, and jogging. She was a rail-thin, gaunt woman, eating on the run and trying to nurse a peptic ulcer at the same time. Dory liked her because she was Griff's mother. Esther's eyes told her that she approved her son's choice. Dory was pleased when they left the restaurant, promising to meet again one day for lunch. It was the kind of promise all busy people make. Some day. Maybe. It wasn't important.

Dory felt annoyed that Esther was coming, but Griff had knocked himself out for Pixie. How could she do less? She couldn't. But, she admonished herself, I don't want to entertain her. Not now, when things are so up in the air, so uncertain. Surely Esther would notice the strain. She might comment and then she might not. She might prefer to let Griff and Dory handle their affairs in their own way without offering advice. She didn't want advice from Esther. From Pixie, yes. Pix would never steer her wrong. Pix could always see both sides of an issue, drunk or sober. Esther would side with her son. Dory knew that Esther wouldn't feel charitable toward her if she thought Dory was casting her son aside.

Her head ached. She rubbed at her temples trying to erase the nagging ache. If anything, it intensified. She could call Esther and tell her she would love to have her for a visit, for a day, but not for a full week. She couldn't handle a week. She would be lucky if she could get through a full day. That's what she should do. But would she do it? Her shoulders stiffened imperceptibly. Griff wouldn't like it if she changed Esther's plans.

I don't want her here. It's going to cause me emotional turmoil, and I have enough going on right now. A call to Griff would settle it. Dory would feel him out, see what he thought.

No, damn it! She wouldn't call Griff, or if she did, it would be to tell him her decision. If he didn't go along with it, that was his problem. Since it was she who would be with Esther most of the time, it should be her decision.

Dory reached for the telephone, punched out Griff's number and waited for the receptionist to put her through.

"Griff, I'm calling about your mother. I plan to call her today but I did want to talk to you first."

"Is something wrong, Dory? Look, if you feel it isn't convenient, cancel out. Mother will understand. Make it for later."

Damn, he was making it too easy. Besides, she didn't want later. She didn't want now, but she was stuck.

"That's just it, Griff. I don't want to make it for later. To be perfectly honest, I don't want to make it for now either. I don't think I can handle your mother for more than two days. Don't be angry. I'm trying to be honest with you. I didn't want to go ahead and call Esther till I spoke to you. She is your mother. But, you're going to be busy with the clinic and I'm the one who will have to entertain her. I don't want to do it, Griff. I can handle two days because I feel that's fair to you and to me. More than that I can't . . ."

"Dory, it's okay with me. You're right. Mom is demanding as a house guest and yes, you're right, you are the one who would have to entertain her. The decision is yours."

"Then you aren't upset with me?"

"Of course not. I know what Mom is like. I understand, Dory," Griff said softly. "Honey, I'm glad that you felt you could be honest with me about all of this. Don't give it another thought."

"It's settled then. I'll call Esther now. See you later, Griff."

It was done. Her second breakthrough. Her second decision. Esther was coming for just the weekend. Dory felt good when she hung up the phone—good about herself. And ready for Esther.

She would have to clean the spare room and change the sheets. She felt as if some kind, wise person had given her a personal reprieve when she yanked sheets and pillow cases out of a drawer. A week ago she would have stewed and fretted over the pattern and probably even ironed the creases. Lily ironed permanent press. But Dory Faraday's ironing days were over. When she was finished she stood back to view her work for neatness. She blinked. The orange and brown zigzag pattern was almost blinding. These had been Griff's sheets. He joked that he had bought them on purpose so they would wake him up in the morning. Esther would certainly be wide eyed.

Dory dusted the furniture with a tissue and blew the dust off the top of the small portable television. As she was leaving the room she contemplated the lint on the carpet. Instead of running the vacuum, she bent down sixteen times to pick up the little bits and pieces of lint. Good for the waistline, she told herself.

When Griff hung up the phone, his mind went blank for a few seconds. The Siamese cat waiting for his gentle touch snoozed peacefully with the aid of a tranquilizer. Damn, his stomach felt as if it was tied in a knot. He didn't like the idea that the two women in his life might be having a problem. His mother could be a pain. If Dory felt she couldn't handle a lengthy visit he could accept that. Hell, he wasn't exactly looking forward to his mother's visit himself. He had to admit, though, that he was surprised by Dory's phone call.

For some reason he had expected her to grin and bear it. He had never known her to dig in her heels and make a decision and then call and announce it to him. Suddenly he laughed. By God, that was exactly what she had done. She didn't ask—she simply told him. It was a good thing. He wasn't stupid. Dory was going through some personal turmoil now and Esther would only crowd the issue. Esther could do that without even trying. He loved his mother but—he grinned down at the sleeping cat—he did his maternal loving better from a distance.

The Siamese opened one eye and looked at the giant towering over him, then rolled over on his side and let the doctor examine him. All thoughts of his mother and Dory fled Griff's mind as he began his careful probing of the ailing animal. Dory had the situation in hand.

Chapter Eleven

GRIFF ARRIVED HOME THAT EVENING RAVENOUSLY HUNGRY. For her. Dinner could wait, he told her with authority. Right now, there were needs food couldn't satisfy.

Dory flushed pink as he wrapped his arms around her, his cheek frigidly cold from the night air, whispering hoarsely into her ear, stirring new yet familiar longings within her.

Dory took Griff by the hand, leading him up to their room, her smile a promise. The fire in their eyes warmed the room as they watched each other undress, readying themselves for the caresses and kisses they hungered for. Griff lowered himself to the bed, gathering her into his arms, burying his lips into the hollow of her throat. Delighted little mewings sounded in her throat when she pressed her face into the furring on his chest, nuzzling at his nipples and feeling him shudder beneath her touch.

"Dory," he breathed, ragged and husky, falling back against the pillows, taking her with him. He found her eager mouth, returning her kisses with a bittersweet ardor. Hers were the softest lips he had ever kissed, and he believed he would never satisfy himself for their touch. His kisses wandered over the planes of her face, in the dimple near her chin, in the shining paleness of her hair.

His hands caressed her body, finding it beautiful as always, and he sighed with contentment as womanly curve fit against manly muscle.

Dory exerted pressure against him, forcing him to his back while she followed, her knees tightly clamped to his sides. She looked down into his adored face, feeling her love for him well inside her. Her long, silver blonde hair created a curtain as she bent to kiss him—long, loving kisses, meant to touch the soul and stir the senses.

Griff smiled up at her when he felt himself being taken within her. This was his Dory, the Dory he loved—always equal, sometimes dominant, sharing the best of herself, the most of herself, making him more a man because she was more a woman.

Their joining was loving, tender, and filled with joy. It had been too long since they had come together this way, equally, hungry for what each could bring to the other instead of that sorry, dispassionate surrender that was a poor balm for a sick spirit.

Sitting in the living room, sharing a glass of wine, Griff told Dory about things at the clinic and listened while she told him about her day in New York. The conversation went from acquaintances in the Big Apple to friends here at the capital.

"What did Sylvia do while I was in New York?" Dory asked. "I suppose she made a raid on Neiman-Marcus."

"Actually, Sylvia is down with the flu. John left early this afternoon to stay with her. He was joking that it's a good thing there are no emergencies at the clinic, otherwise it would all fall to me. Sometimes John and I regret the deal we made with Rick that he'd never have to work evenings. He always shows up extra early at the clinic, and he's no slouch on the job, so I suppose it all evens out in the end."

"Rick never stays late?" Dory asked, thinking of the last time she was with Lily and how despondent she had seemed. If memory served her, Lily had said that Rick would definitely be working late that particular evening. Dory also remembered the oncoming anxiety attack she'd suffered when she realized that if domestic, all-giving, Lily wasn't safe, then no one was. Safe. What a funny word, Dory thought as she nestled down into the curve of Griff's arm. Still, when

she thought of making her decision and calling Lizzie on
Monday, she wanted to actually crawl inside Griff, have him
make the decision for her. She would like it if he would tell
her what to do, take the responsibility away from her. Be one
of those arrogant, chauvinistic men her mother was always
reading about in romantic novels. Dory took another sip of
wine, feeling it cool against her tongue. She hadn't told Griff
about having to make that call on Monday and now she was
glad she hadn't. This was one decision she'd have to live with
the rest of her life, and it was one she was going to be totally
responsible for. For the first time in a long while Dory finally
felt good about herself. That didn't make the decision any
easier, and she knew it, but she still felt good.

Dory was misting the fresh evergreen and the plants when
she saw a taxi pull up in front of the town house and a
mink-cloaked woman emerge, looking up at the house number.
Griff's mother.

Esther Michaels arrived carrying a poinsettia plant that
Dory could only describe as regal. Poinsettias were by nature
full and leafy with bright scarlet leaves; Esther's plant grew
straight up like a tree. She carried it as though she were the
Olympic torch bearer. A Neiman-Marcus shopping bag and one
from Gucci were clutched in her free hand. The taxi driver set
her pullman bag down in the kitchen and waited patiently
while Esther settled the plant and her shopping bags. She
counted out the exact amount from a small change purse and
added a skimpy gratuity.

"Merry Christmas to you too, lady," the driver said sourly
as he slammed the back door behind him.

"What was that all about?" Esther asked frigidly, honestly
perplexed. "He gets paid by the company he works for,
doesn't he?"

Dory eyed the large pullman. Just how long would Esther
be staying? Maybe she was joining Pixie halfway around the
world. The ridiculous thought almost choked her. This imperi-
ous woman would hardly acknowledge someone like Pixie,
much less travel with her. Now, that isn't fair, Dory old girl.

Esther is a lovely person; quit thinking these shabby thoughts about the poor woman. Nuts, she told herself.

"It looks as though you've been shopping," Dory said, hoping to ease the conversation into a light pattern, anything to get Mrs. Michaels to loosen up and make the visit bearable. Clearly, having dinner in the city with Griff's mother was quite different from having her come to stay.

"Christmas presents for you and Griffin. I do so like the holidays, and I'm so glad you invited me. I was afraid I'd be excluded from my son's Christmas," she said as she slipped out of her twenty-year-old mink that, unbelievably, was coming back into style because of its straight lines and wide Joan Crawford shoulders. "How is Griffin?" Esther asked as she removed her powder-puff mink hat and patted at her silvery hair. She looked lacquered, Dory assessed, and she would stake her life that Esther was a product of Elizabeth Arden . . . five days a week with pedicures thrown in. She was perfectly groomed from the top of her sleek French twist to the tip of her shoes.

"Griff's fine. He's working very hard to make the clinic a success. They all are, John and Rick included. Sometimes I think he does more than his share, but he's doing what he wants and what he likes best. That's what's important," Dory said quietly, mentally calculating the cost of Esther's Oleg Cassini suit. She'd been hanging around Sylvia too much!

Esther's look was sharp as she confronted Dory. She had just taken a really good look at the young woman. This couldn't be the same Dory she had met for lunches in the city, or could it? Griffin, dear boy, what have we here? Good lord, Dory's cheeks stopped just short of being plump. Esther's eye skimmed down Dory's figure, focusing on the waistline which was concealed beneath the lilac sweatshirt she wore. Was there a grandchild in the making? What did Griffin think of this? Where was the chic, the elegance, the success of Dory Faraday that had so attracted Griffin and had so pleased her?

Esther would not be a snob. Griffin hated snobbery. Still . . . this young woman, and she wasn't *that* young . . . something was definitely amiss. She could sense it. She hoped her tone was light when she replied, "Griffin has had this dream ever since he was a small boy. He's worked hard and I'm so proud of him. I do love winners, you know, Dory." It was on the tip of her tongue to ask if Dory's suspected pregnancy was a fact, but Esther bit back the words. She would ask Griff. She didn't want Dory to think that a grandchild was eagerly anticipated. It wasn't. And should suspicion become reality, Esther knew she'd be hard pressed to hide her disappointment.

Dory nodded. She should be verbally agreeing with Esther, but it was hard to concentrate. Esther kept staring at her as if she were a bug on the end of a pin. She knew that in the past ten minutes she had failed miserably in Esther's eyes. She didn't measure up. She came up short. A lump settled in her throat. Damn it, why did people always have to judge other people? Why couldn't they just accept them?

Esther's tone became fretful. Lord, was she really going to have to stay here for an entire weekend? What *would* they do? The scent of the pine boughs and the giant tree was making her nauseous. Why couldn't they have had a plastic tree like everyone else? And all those decorations. God! Elves, gnomes, reindeer, and a lot of little stuffed mice. God! She forced a smile to her lips, lips that Dory knew were painted with a brush. The eyelashes came out of a case. Dory wished the bright blue gaze weren't so piercing, so probing. Lord, surely she wasn't waiting for confidences. The thought was so horrific, Dory almost gagged.

"Esther, would you care for a drink? Coffee? Soft drink? Brandy?" Damn, there wasn't any brandy; Pix drank it all. Please don't ask for brandy. There wasn't any scotch either; Pix finished that the day she left. Her eyes tried to probe the liquor cabinet to see what there was. Vodka, gin, and some bourbon.

"Do you have any Diet Pepsi?"

Dory stared at Esther. Diet Pepsi. Of course, she would ask for Diet Pepsi. Pixie's experience with Diet Pepsi made her laugh aloud. Esther stared at her, frowning. "Private joke,"

169

Dory mumbled as she got up to get the drink for Griff's mother.

An hour later Esther said she felt tired and perhaps a warm bath and a tiny little nap might be in order. Dory almost killed herself getting up from the couch to show Esther the way to her room.

Back in the kitchen she sat with her hands propped under her chin. I don't need this. I don't want this. This visit isn't making me happy. And what are you going to do about it? her friend the inner voice chided. Not much, Dory grimaced. I'm temporarily stuck. After all, she is Griff's mother and I have . . . I want . . .

Damn, the holidays with all the pressures were getting to be a bore. The word startled Dory. A bore? It was true. Everything of late was a bore. And, I'm the biggest bore of all. The mental statement of fact did nothing for her mood.

When life and everyone in it was a bore there was only one thing to do. Dory stretched full length on the sofa. She pressed the ON button on the remote control. A soap opera sprung to life. Ha! And they thought they had problems. Within seconds, Dory was asleep.

The next two days were torture for Dory. Griff seemed to creep about, and Esther kept looking at Dory out of the corner of her eye. Dory couldn't wait for Esther to leave, and Esther couldn't wait to be gone. Griff kept looking at the two women in his life with puzzled expressions. Christmas Eve came and went with carols on the television and the opening of gifts. Nothing seemed to faze Dory. Christmas Day was dinner and a scrumptious dessert that only Griff ate.

Esther packed her bags while Dory cleaned the kitchen and Griff watched someone's family on television tell what their Christmas was like. B-o-r-i-n-g.

When Griff returned from the airport, he stalked into the kitchen. "If you don't mind, would you tell me just what the hell is going on. What went on here? What in the hell has happened to you, Dory?"

Dory stared at Griff. He had never spoken to her like this

before. Damn, put a man's mother into the picture and it was a whole new ball game. Was he taking sides?

"I wish you had warned me what a pain in the neck your mother was. Two or three lunches weren't enough time to get to know her. And what gives you the right to talk to me that way? I'm not your wife, you know," Dory said bluntly.

Griff slumped down on the sofa, his red muffler with the missed stitches, Dory's first effort, still around his neck. His voice was soft, too soft, when he spoke. "I know that. I mean about you not being my wife. Even if you were, I had no right to blast off like that. I'm sorry."

"I guess I am too."

"You guess, don't you know?" Griff said coldly.

"No, I guess I don't know for sure. Everything is all mixed up. I feel so confused, Griff. I've been wanting to talk to you for weeks now, but you're always busy or tired or something."

"What's that supposed to mean?"

"It means whatever you want it to mean. Something's wrong, Griff, can't you feel it? Can't you see it?"

"Something's been wrong for a long time. I've been waiting for you to get your act together so we could discuss it. I'm not that busy. Every time I want to talk to you, you're making bread or cookies or sewing or some damn thing. If you aren't doing that, you're on the phone with Lily or Sylvia. What am I supposed to think? The next thing you'll be getting headaches and backaches."

"That was a low thing to say," Dory snapped.

"It's true, isn't it? I damn near knocked myself out for your aunt when she was here. I had every right to expect you to do the same for my mother."

"I did. Is it my fault she doesn't want to go outside because her makeup will crack, and is it my fault that she has ulcers and can't eat regular food, and is it my fault that her last two accounts fell through, and is it my fault that I didn't know where her church was, a church that she attends once a year? Don't hang any guilt trips on me, Griff. The whole time she was here she kept staring at me as though I were some-

171

thing that should be under a microscope. I've had enough guilt to last me a lifetime. My aunt asked nothing of you; she didn't put you out, and she went out of her way to be extremely generous to both of us. If you didn't like her, why don't you just say so? No more guilt, you've given me enough trips that if I laid them end to end I could go to the moon. I've had enough!''

"So have I!'' Griff yelled back.

Tears burned Dory's eyes. It shouldn't be happening like this. They should be talking it out like the sensible adults they were. She dropped to her knees in front of Griff and grasped both of his hands in hers. "I'm sorry, Griff, this is all my fault. This . . . this fight we're having is something that bubbled up and got out of hand. In a way, I suppose I subconsciously wanted it this way so I could . . . what I mean is . . . I thought it would make it easier for me to say what I have to say.''

She drew a deep breath and held up her hand to silence him. "Please, Griff, let me say what I have to say because if I don't I may never get the nerve again. This was wrong for all the right reasons. I wasn't ready to make a commitment to you, either in a relationship or in marriage. I came here with you telling myself that I was going to go back to school. I wasn't even truthful with myself. Oh, in the beginning I believed it, at least for a little while. I copped out is what I did. With school, with you, and with myself. I tried to be like Sylvia because I thought that was what you wanted. Then I tried to be like Lily because I saw the approving way you looked at her. When that didn't work out, I tried to be a combination of both of them, thinking I read you wrong. What I didn't ever do was be myself. I'm not Susy Home-maker and I'm not a social butterfly. I'm me. I lost sight of that for a while. I'm not perfect but I'm all I've got and I have to get me back while I can. I'm not a loser, Griff. I don't even want to be a winner, I just want to be me. I have to go back and pick up my pieces.''

"I know,'' Griff said huskily. "I know.''

Warm tears trickled down Dory's cheeks. "I love you, Griff."

"And I love you."

"I'll only be an hour away. We can still see each other. I can write or call."

"I can do the same."

It was a lie and they both knew it.

"It took nerve for you to wear that muffler out in public, especially to the airport," Dory said, wiping at her tears.

"You're telling me. I lost track of the people who turned around to stare at me. Come here, Dory."

His arms wrapped around her. Her haven. Her warmth. Her security. She didn't have to let go. She could hang on and maybe some day. . . .

"No regrets, Dory," Griff said, smoothing the tangled hair back from her forehead. "You gave it your best shot and so did I. It wasn't meant to be . . . for now, anyway." There was a long pause. "When will you leave?" Griff asked.

Without a second's hesitation, Dory replied, "In the morning. I'll stay in Katy's spare room till my sublet leaves."

Griff tilted Dory's head back so that he could meet her tear-filled gaze. "It's right for you. If you hadn't made the decision, I would have made it for you. I'm proud of you, Dory."

"Oh, Griff, I do love you. I hope I can handle this. Help me, please." She burrowed into his chest, her sobs racking her body. If it was this hard now, what was it going to be like when she got back to the city and was alone? Griff held her close, stroking her hair and her back.

He held her through the long night, his arms and back numb with the pressure of her body, but he didn't move. He watched the fire die down and then he watched the smoldering ashes. The twinkling lights of the Christmas tree were the only light once the embers turned to feathery, light dust.

As dawn crept up Griff shifted his weight on the sofa, his grip secure on the sleeping woman in his arms. "Almost time to leave the nest," he murmured.

His eyes smarted. From the smoke in the fireplace, no

doubt. And the lump in his throat, his mouth was dry. The night had been long and his throat was parched.

She felt so good, so right in his arms. He had to let her go. She needed to go. He knew that one word, one look from him and she'd stay. He loved her too much to do that to her. In the end she would grow to hate him. He would hate himself.

"Time to fly, little bird," he said softly as he tried to move his arms. Dory stirred sleepily and then was instantly awake. She smiled. The first dazzling smile he had seen on her face since they moved here. His heart ached for what might have been.

"Griff, the tree, all the decorations . . ."

"I'll have one of the boys from the clinic pack everything away. While you get your things together what say I make us a going-away breakfast."

"Sounds good to me. Most of my things have been packed for some time. Griff, don't make more of that statement than there is."

"I won't."

Griff's movements in the kitchen were sluggish. He hated what he was doing. He hated farewells. He hated good-bys of any kind.

Dory sat down to black toast and brown scrambled eggs. It was the most delicious food she had ever tasted. "Let's not make any promises or play any games, Griff."

"Agreed."

"We'll keep in touch. If you're ever in the city . . . if I ever find myself here . . . you know. Tell Sylvia and Lily I'll drop them a note."

"Gotcha," Griff said, forcing a light note into his voice.

A horn sounded outside. The taxi. Dory looked at Griff. "I didn't want you to take me to the airport. I wanted to leave you here, so I could think of you this way, not among strangers in a sterile airport. I have to go, Griff," she whispered, choking back a sob.

"I know, Dory love. You need to be back in your own climate, in your own environment. It's where you thrive, where you like yourself to be."

"I like to be in your arms, Griff. That's where I like to be. But it's not enough."

"I love you, Dory. Hurry, cab drivers aren't known for their patience."

"Griff . . ."

"I know, love. I know."

"I love you, Griff."

"And I love you. Move, damn it, or this is all going to be for nothing, and we'll have to replay it all when the next cab comes to get you." The sound of the horn pierced the frigid air outside.

Without another word, without another glance, Dory turned and walked out the door.

Griff stood by the window long after the taxi had gone. She was going back to her world. She was gone. He felt like hell. Probably a cold coming on. He was overdue.

Maybe he should go over to Rick and Lily's to have coffee and tell them that Dory was gone. Lily would be feeding the baby about this time.

Griff blew his nose lustily. For sure, it was a cold. What else could it be?

Chapter Twelve

Dory had put in her first week of work on the job and she knew she had made the right decision. Life was exciting again; she accepted her share of stress and plunged herself into learning Lizzie's managerial duties. Soon, she hoped, she would be able to blend those managerial skills with her own brand of creativeness, and her job would be innovative as well as challenging.

So what if this particular brand of happiness was paid for by crying herself to sleep every night? So what if her appetite was less than it should be and every pair of broad shoulders and head of dark hair she noticed in a crowd seemed to be Griff? She was coping. She was handling it better than she had expected. That was all that mattered, she told herself. As Pixie often said, "Everything in life has a price. The trick is deciding if you want to pay it."

The door to her office opened and in stepped David Harlow. "Katy said you'd need this coffee about now." He sat a cup that boasted "BEST BOSS IN TOWN" down on her desk. "You look tired, so I guess she was right. I stopped by to invite you out for dinner." There was a gleam in his eye as he appraised her sleek shining hair that brushed the shoulders of her mauve silk blouse. With a proprietary air, he reached out to smooth the pale blonde strands.

Dory backed away. "Sorry, Mr. Harlow, I can't make it." She leaned back in her chair, sipping the fragrant brew.

"When we're alone you're to call me David," he told her, his tone oily. "How about tomorrow?"

"Busy, Mr. Harlow. In case you're not getting the message, I will call you Mr. Harlow." Dory placed the cup on her desk and stood up to face him.

She stood tall, smoothing her skirt over her hips. "Let me tell you something, Mr. Harlow. I am well aware of the fact that you have it in your power to remove me from the ranks of *Soiree*. Before I made my decision to return here, I knew that there would never be anything between the two of us, and I'm prepared to start over again somewhere else. I will not be compromised."

Harlow spoke as though he hadn't heard a word Dory had said. "What about dinner Saturday or Sunday? We can take in jai alai in Connecticut."

Dory shook her head.

"When won't you be busy?"

Dory flinched at his tone. This was it. "You're not listening to me, Mr. Harlow. It's time we understood one another. If you and what you're suggesting goes with this job, then you have the wrong woman. Oh, I could make all kinds of threats about going to the Civil Liberties Union or yelling sexual harassment, but I'm going to get on with my life, and I'm not going to let you get under my skin. I'll simply clean out my desk and be out of here within the hour. That, Mr. Harlow, is the bottom line. Take it or leave it." There, she had said it and she knew he'd been listening. And it hadn't been as difficult as she'd thought. She kept her gaze steady and waited.

Harlow grinned wolfishly and held out his hand. He was whipped and he knew it, and wasn't it said that discretion was the better part of valor? There were other girls, less dedicated women who could appreciate a man like himself. Oh, he knew he wasn't much to look at, but he also knew something else. Women were attracted to power. An Adonis of a janitor couldn't compete with the homeliest of men who held the three "P's": power, position and persistence. "Well, they

177

told me you weren't a pushover, Dory.'' He grinned broadly. "This is only a truce; it doesn't mean I won't keep trying.''

"Just so the record is straight,'' Dory told him firmly. "And also for the record, if you're Mr. Harlow, then I'm Ms. Faraday. Got it?'' She extended her hand for a shake.

"You have style, Faraday, I'll give you that.''

"That's what they tell me. Time to get back to work, Harlow. Thanks for stopping by.''

Harlow grinned. "Next time I'll make an appointment.''

"Do that.'' Dory grinned back.

Harlow left her office, but he winked at her before he left. She wanted to throw something at him. He'd said the words and played the scene, but he hadn't believed a word of it. As far as he was concerned, Dory was simply going to take a little longer than other women. But even with her anger, Dory knew a satisfaction. She'd played by her own rules, and while she hadn't exactly had a complete victory, the ball was in her court. David Harlow would probably always be a thorn in her side but she'd cope. It was going to be rocky, but she'd been over rough turf before.

There was one more thing to do before she could sit back and relax with Pixie's letter, which had arrived in the morning mail. And then back to Katy's comfortable ranch house on the Island.

She flipped through the rolodex till she found the number she wanted, then dialed and waited.

"Senator Collins' office. May I help you?''

"Dory Faraday, Miss Oliver. Is the senator in?''

"One moment please.''

"Ah, Miss Faraday, it's a pleasure to hear your voice at the end of a long day, a very long day.''

"Thank you.'' There was that smile in his voice again. "Senator, I really do want to apologize for not getting together over the holidays. I moved back to the city and managed to get myself promoted in the bargain. I think I more or less have things squared away here. How's your schedule?''

"Hectic. But, I have a farm in McLean where I go weekends.

By pure chance I happen to have the next four free. I have to warn you, though, that could change at any time. For now, it's good for me if you could manage to get down here.''

Dory's heart picked up an extra beat as she contemplated a long weekend with the man who owned such a wonderful voice. "I think I can arrange it. Would you like to start this weekend?''

"It's all right with me. Just tell me your flight number and I'll have someone pick you up at the airport.''

"I'll get back to your secretary tomorrow, Senator. I'm looking forward to working with you on this project. I think it's going to be one of our better political profiles.'' As she spoke, Dory riffled through the files in the bottom right-hand drawer of her desk. Where was the envelope Katy had sent her with that material on Drake Collins? She had been so involved with making her decisions that she'd never opened it.

Her fingers found the mailing envelope and she pulled the tab to open it. Senator Collins was talking about bringing a pair of warm boots and heavy sweaters to the farm. She'd have to follow him around while he tended to chores and he planned to do some riding. Did she ride?

The contents of the envelope scattered out onto Dory's desk. There were newspaper clippings, Xeroxed copies of magazine articles in *Fortune, Business Week*, and *Time*. And an 8 x 10 black-and-white glossy photo, no doubt from the senator's campaign. Dory picked up the photo. Laughing eyes looked back into hers from a handsome face. Dory's eyes widened. The man at the airport. The senator was the man at the airport who had picked up her dropped glove and had wanted to take her for coffee! Little bubbles of excitement fizzed through her blood. There had been an instant attraction between them. She knew it; any woman could instantly tell if a man was interested in her.

"I'm counting on this article for *Soiree* to assure me of being a shoo-in on my next campaign for office," the senator quipped.

"We do have an astronomical circulation in your home

179

state, Senator. If nothing else, you'll have the edge over your opponent.''

"I'm looking forward to your visit. Till Saturday," Drake Collins signed off.

Dory sat for a long time staring at the phone. It was incredible, simply incredible. It would be fun to see if the senator recognized her from the airport. Fun. That was what she wanted right now. She still wasn't over Griff, and she didn't expect to be for a long, long time. She wondered what he was doing right now, this minute. She glanced at her watch. He'd still be at the clinic. Would he eat supper alone? With someone? Was he eating right?

Dory's shoulders slumped. She shouldn't be worrying about him this way. But love, when it died, died hard. And Dory still loved Griff, in a very special way. More special because Griff recognized her needs and was unselfish enough to think of Dory first. If anyone had had doubts or qualms about Dory moving to Washington, it had been Griff. He'd wanted to marry her. Perhaps marriage would have made the difference. There would have been a commitment. She would have had to think things through very carefully. Dory realized now that she had never burned her bridges behind her when she left New York. She had purposely contrived to keep a spot open for herself in case she wanted to return. But then, why had she left in the first place? Was it plain weariness of job and stress? Was it because she realized Lizzie would be leaving and she'd been the most natural person to step into the job? Did she think at the time that she couldn't handle the position? Was that why running away with Griff had seemed so important? And that was what it had been, running away, knowing that *Soiree* would welcome back its prodigal child.

She loved Griff, yet she had used him. In return for all those household chores and making a home, she had expected safety and solace. And still it hadn't been there for her. No sooner had she arrived than she had begun to worry that Griff didn't love her, didn't admire her, that he'd admired other women more. She had expected to *keep* a home for Griff, but she had also expected him to *make* a home for her. Foolish girl. Why and where had she gotten the idea that all things good and worth having come to a woman only through a man? Griff hadn't changed, *she* had! Griff hadn't expected her to sacrifice, she had simply done it. He hadn't asked . . . she had simply given. And always he had appreciated it, but probably the whole time he'd wondered where his Dory had gone. The Dory he had known in New York and had fallen in love with.

"Griff . . . Griff . . . I let both of us down, didn't I?" She looked at the phone. She'd finally gotten it all straight in her own head and she wanted to tell Griff. Her hand fell back into her lap and she laughed aloud. Griff knew. Griff had always known.

Dory blinked back a tear, a smile forming on her lips. For now, she had found the place she needed to be, to grow. It wasn't the answer to everything in her life, but until she *wanted* to be somewhere else, it was home. And she was home free.

On to bigger and better things. Better things like a letter from Pixie. The airmail paper was as crisp and crackly as celery. Dory smoothed out the pages and leaned back, her feet propped up on an open drawer. It paid to be comfortable when starting one of Pixie's letters.

Dory, Sweet Child,

I know you must be chewing your nails wondering how I'm doing. In a word, super. That's as in s-u-p-e-r! Mr. Cho (he insists I call him Mr. Cho) and I are a perfect match. I've already filled the journal you gave me for Christmas. There was a tricky moment or two when Mr. Cho wanted to know why I had so many names. I glossed over the whole thing and he now thinks all Americans are crazy. Wealthy and crazy!

I'm marrying Mr. Cho on the second day of the Chinese New Year which is shortly after ours. He's a remarkable man. As you know, he demanded a dowry. He also demanded all my assets and said he would retire to manage them. We've worked up a written contract whereby he agrees to devote his entire life to me and to make you and me all the shoes we can

181

hope to wear in a lifetime. (I had to fight for that one.) We both know I have a tendency to be flaky, but I have never been one to buy a pig in the poke. We did a little plea bargaining which is another way of saying I demanded a sample of his devotion. My dear, may I say it was one of the most heady experiences of my life. I worried for naught. I think even Mr. Cho was startled. We had a bit of a role reversal when I had to wait for him for two days before he could get it all together. I loved every minute of it. I felt so . . . so . . . lecherous.

Mr. Cho is thirty-nine years old. I was a little surprised but he said not to concern myself, that age was only a number. He constantly tells me I'm a work of art, meaning, I'm sure, that I'm a treasure.

Mr. Cho will retire officially the day of our marriage. The nuptial agreement has many little clauses and tacky little promises that I have no intention of honoring. I'm contributing seventy-five thousand dollars to the marriage. If Mr. Cho's eyes weren't almond shaped, I think they would have widened in surprise. He considers that amount equal to being a millionaire. Aren't you proud of me? I never give all of everything except my body. Mr. Cho loves my wigs. He's now trying to figure out a way to keep them from slipping off my head. He loves to run his fingers through them. (Is that kinky or is that kinky?) On my arrival we both got blitzed, me on his rice wine and he on my scotch. It was memorable.

I plan to take up residence in his house in Aberdeen. I'll have cards made up and send you one. Actually, the house is a shack. One of these days when I'm not too busy I may fix it up. Hong Kong is magnificent, and I do my shopping in Kowloon. Mr. Cho barters and haggles for me so no one loses face.

Under separate cover I'm sending you all the materials Mr. Cho requires for a mold of both your feet. Rush it back to me. I don't want him to get too lazy. Devotion is the name of the game, and if I'm paying for it, I want "our" money's worth.

I'd write more but Mr. Cho is suffering his third relapse

*and I want to make him some rum tea. These Orientals have
no stamina. I can't even begin to tell you the trouble I had
when I tried to explain the word 'performance' to him. Now
he understands. That's why he's working on his third relapse.
Just last night I had to tell him my bankers weren't going to
be too happy if he kept caving in on a regular basis. Poor
darling, every time I say, "up, up and away," he turns
green.*

*Dory, dear child, I hope all is well with you and that you
have made decisions of your own. I'm sending this letter to
the magazine. I didn't want your mother getting hold of it. I
can just see and hear her clucking her tongue and saying
"that damn fool, he married her for her money." I know it's
true and you know it's true, but your mother doesn't need to
know. I can live with my deicisions because for the first time
in thirty years I'm happy doing what I want when I want.
Amazing that I had to come halfway around the world to do
it. Well almost, I do have to consider Mr. Cho and his . . .
ah . . . slight deficiency. See if you can't get me one of those
sex manuals that deals with staying power. Rush it airmail in
a plain brown wrapper.*

*One last thing, Dory. After my seventy-five thousand dollar
withdrawal, I signed my power of attorney over to you. I
don't want those articulate bankers on my tail. Do whatever
you have to do where my affairs are concerned.*

Take care, Dory, and please, be happy for me.

*All my love and good wishes,
Aunt Pixie*

Tears burned Dory's eyes as she folded the crackly letter.
"Right on, Pix," she said softly. "Right on." There were
many kinds of happiness, she told herself as she slid the letter
into the desk drawer. Coming back was her kind.

How many times had she thought about Griff today,
yesterday, the day before that? Hundreds? Thousands? At
least. Why not call him? They'd had so much. She couldn't

just cut it off. Why not call him and ask how he was doing? Why hadn't he called to ask her how she was doing? Because he was a man and a man didn't do things like that. Besides, she was the one who walked out. Before she could change her mind she dialed the number at the town house. Griff answered on the third ring.

His voice was just as she remembered and it did the same things to her it had always done. Her heart fluttered a little and her tongue felt as if it were stuck to the roof of her mouth. "Hi," she said brightly.

"Hi yourself. I was just thinking of you."

"Oh, how's that?"

"Because I just got done eating a casserole you had frozen. It was delicious. You left enough food to last me a month."

"I'm glad you're eating properly."

"So am I. How's things in New York."

"Pretty good. I'm busy as hell but I love it. I got a letter from Pixie today. There's no way I can tell you what all she had to say. I could make a copy and send it on if you'd like to read it."

"I'd like that. Please, send me a copy. Jesus, are you listening to the both of us. We sound so polite, so bland, so . . . so . . ."

"Like two nerds," Dory laughed.

"Yeah. I was going to call you but then I told myself you needed the time to get back into the swing of things. I want you to believe that."

"Why wouldn't I? You never lied to me, Griff. I think of you constantly. On the hour at least."

"I know, I do the same thing," Griff said gruffly. "Look, what are you doing two weeks from Friday? I thought I'd come up and we could do the town or whatever you want. I could bring your things back then too. Lily said she would pack everything up this week."

"I'd like that Griff, I really would."

"Okay, it's a date then unless Starfire foals that day. Can we leave it on that basis?"

"Sure. How's things at the clinic?"

"Great. We have more business than we can handle. Thinking of taking on a fourth partner. John fired Ginny today for no reason. Just out and out sacked her. Since he's the senior partner there wasn't much either Rick or I could do. For some reason it bothered Rick. By the way, Rick tells me Lily thinks she's pregnant again. He seems delighted and Lily of course is bubbling over with happiness."

Dory swallowed hard. "That . . . that's wonderful. What are you going to do about the town house?"

"I don't need this much room. It's pretty expensive. Lily said she'd get me an efficiency apartment so I kind of left it up to her. I can't stay here," Griff groaned. "There are too many memories. It's the wise thing to do."

"Yes." She hated to ask it but she had to know. "Are you . . . are you seeing anyone?"

"The only lady in my life right now is Starfire. How about you?"

"No. I've been pretty busy."

"I've missed you. You wouldn't believe the condition of the bathroom. You'd kill me if you saw it."

Dory laughed. "I wish I was there to see it."

"I know you do. This . . . this conversation isn't helping either of us, I guess you know that," Griff said hoarsely.

"You're right. I'll look forward to seeing you in two weeks. And Griff, if Starfire foals, there will be other weekends."

"See you, Dory."

"I'm counting on it," Dory said as she hung up the phone.

A smile tugged at her mouth as she circled the date with a red pencil. Next to it she wrote in large letters: GRIFF.

Dear Reader:

Your opinions are important to us so please take a few moments to tell us your thoughts. It will help us give you more enjoyable LOVE & LIFE Books in the future.

1. Where did you obtain this book?

Bookstore	☐ 1	Newsstand	☐ 6	5
Supermarket	☐ 2	Airport	☐ 7	
Variety/discount store	☐ 3	From A Friend	☐ 8	
Department store	☐ 4	Other_____		
Drug store	☐ 5	(write in)		

2. On an overall basis, how would you rate this book?

Excellent ☐ 1   Good ☐ 3   Poor ☐ 5   6
Very Good ☐ 2   Fair ☐ 4

3. What did you like best about this book?

Heroine ☐ 1 Hero ☐ 2 Setting ☐ 3 Storyline ☐ 4   7
Love scenes ☐ 5 Ending ☐ 6 Other Characters ☐ 7

4. Do you prefer love scenes that are

Less explicit than   More explicit than
  in this book ☐ 1   in this book ☐ 2   8
      About as explicit as in this book ☐ 3

5. How likely would you be to purchase other LOVE & LIFE Editions in the future?

Extremely likely ☐ 1   Not very likely ☐ 3   9
Somewhat likely ☐ 2   Not at all likely ☐ 4

6. Please indicate your age group.

Under 18 ☐ 1   25-34 ☐ 3   50 or older ☐ 5   10
18-24   ☐ 2   35-49 ☐ 4

If you would like a free subscription to the LOVE & LIFE Romance Newsletter, please fill in your name and address.

NAME_____

ADDRESS_____

CITY_____ STATE_____ ZIP CODE_____   11

Please mail to: Ballantine Books
                 LOVE & LIFE Research Dept.
                 516 Fifth Avenue—Suite 606
                 New York, N.Y. 10036

L-18